BLACK *IN* BLUE

NyRee Ausler

D1365185

PenWrite

BLACK IN BLUE | NYREE AUSLER

TABLE OF CONTENTS

BLACK IN BLUE | NYREE AUSLER

PROLOGUE

"Drop the gun!" Chance took aim at the man.

"You drop *your* gun!" he responded. He pressed the barrel of the 9mm to the woman's temple. Tears ran down her face and her legs wobbled.

"Honey, please! Don't do this!" she pleaded.

"Don't call me honey now! I wasn't your honey when you were sleeping with him, was I?" he spat. He slammed the butt of the gun against the top of her head, opening a deep gash. A crimson red stream ran down her forehead. She blinked repeatedly to remove the red blur from her eyes.

Chance squeezed his hands around his weapon tightly. Droplets of perspiration accumulated on his forehead. He didn't have a clean shot, but there was no way he was going to let this guy walk out of here with a hostage.

"What's your name?" he asked the man.

"None of your fucking business!"

"Look, I want to help you. Nobody has to get hurt here, okay?"

The disheveled man threw his head back in laughter. "Yeah, right! You cops aren't here to help me. You're here to kill me and save her!" He pulled the woman closer, almost putting her in a headlock.

"I don't want to hurt you, man. What's your name, bro?" Chance repeated.

There was an awkward silence as the suspect contemplated whether or not it was a good idea to give his name. Chance waited patiently. He didn't care about the man's name, but as long as he could keep him talking, he wasn't shooting the young lady.

Just when he was starting to wonder if things were about to go left, Rocky appeared on the balcony behind the man. Careful not to divert his attention and let on that the captor had lost his advantage, Chance kept his eyes trained on the man, but used one hand to scratch the tip of his nose. He and Rocky had been here on numerous occasions and they both knew that was the signal to hold off. There was still a possibility that the man would cooperate.

Rocky, stay cool! Give me a second to work on him! Chance silently pleaded. His partner had always had an itchy trigger finger and the last thing they needed right now was another internal affairs investigation.

"Tim," the man suddenly blurted out, catching Chance off guard. The tense moment had lasted so long, he almost forgot he'd even asked a question.

Chance cleared his throat. "Okay, Tim. Tell me what you want. How can we end this without anyone getting hurt?"

Tim burst into tears. "I just want my family back. I want my wife and kids."

Dammit! Chance really needed him to stay in control of his emotions. "Tim, I'm sure we can sit down and talk about it after this is all over."

"We can't talk about anything!" he yelled. "She's got me on a restraining order. I haven't seen my kids in months. And to top it off she got married to another dude!"

"T-Ti-Tim... I will divorce him and come back to you. I promise!" she blubbered.

He yanked her head back by her ponytail and placed his mouth to her ear. "You liar! You think you can play games with me?"

Shut up, ma'am! "Tim, talk to me. Think about your kids, man. Let's make sure they still have both parents. You don't want them to lose their mother, do you?"

Tim's breathing was labored as he considered the question. The red dot from Rocky's weapon danced along the side of his head. Chance said a silent prayer that the man would finally surrender.

Just when it seemed that there would be no resolution, Tim said, "If I give up, will you make sure I get to see my kids?"

"I promise, Tim. Trust me," the woman begged.

Everyone held their breath as he made his decision. Finally, he started to slowly lower his gun from her temple. She seemed uncertain as he nudged her toward Chance. She moved forward gingerly.

"Tim, can you please throw your weapon on the ground?" Chance silently pleaded for the man to obey

"I ain't gonna shoot anybody. I'm letting her go," he explained.

"I understand that, but I have to have you lower your weapon to be sure my team knows that you're cooperating." He nodded in the direction of the balcony and Tim spotted Rocky out of the corner of his eye.

Tim groaned, well aware that unless he dropped his weapon, he would not make it out of this situation alive. "Fine." He aimed the weapon away from Chance and the woman and extended his arm, offering the gun up.

The woman trembled and took tiny steps forward. "Tim, please don't shoot me," she cried.

"Tim's fine. He's not going to shoot anyone," Chance assured her. "Everything is fine. Tell me your name."

"Susan. Susan Collins."

"Listen, Susan. No one is going to get shot here, you understand me? We are all going to be okay."

She nodded and used her sleeve to wipe the blood and tears from her face.

Tim seemed to be calmer than he was initially. He sobbed quietly.

"Keep moving toward me, Susan," Chance directed as he cautiously approached.

Tim's body language told him that he would be able to apprehend him without incident.

"Just a few more steps, Susan."

"Okay," she said as she forced a smile.

As he was about to intercept her, Tim shifted and took a step forward to give up the gun.

"Don't move!" Chance shouted. But it was too late.

The whiz of two bullets sliced through the air and Tim's body jerked violently as they struck him. As he lost control of his reflexes, his arm jerked upward and his finger squeezed the trigger. Things seemed to be moving in slow motion as the woman's chest exploded and she lurched forward, collapsing to the ground.

"No!" Chance screamed, as he dropped to his knees next to the woman. He could tell it was too late to help her or Tim.

Rocky stepped through the now shattered sliding glass door and into the room, his rifle still smoking from the shots he had discharged. He and Chance stared at each other, both understanding the gravity of what had just taken place.

THE THIN BLUE LINE

Chance took one last glance at Rocky as they were both ushered into separate cars. Officers from a neighboring jurisdiction had shown up to handle the investigation per protocol.

The images of Tim and his ex-wife both being shot right before his eyes played over and over again in Chance's mind. He couldn't believe Rocky had shot the man. He was giving up. He thought about the children that would be left behind by the senseless murder of both parents. Chance blinked back tears as they pulled into the station.

Okay, Chance. No flip-flopping. No uncertainty. You have to be confident and straight-forward. Get a hold of yourself. Rocky was wrong to shoot. There was no question about that. But, there was also no way Chance could throw him under the bus. His career and his freedom were on the line. He had saved Chance's life on more than one occasion. *What good will it do to be honest?* He asked himself. *It's not like it'll bring Tim and Susan back.*

"Good afternoon, Officer Carrington," the lieutenant greeted. He gestured toward the empty chair and Chance took a seat. "I appreciate your meeting to discuss this incident."

Chance almost scoffed at the suggestion that any of this was voluntary. He would rather be anywhere else in the world than in this room at this very moment.

As the lieutenant set up his recording device and prepared his questions, Chance looked around the room.

1

The gray stone walls made him feel caged in and the cold steel of the metal table that his clasped hands rested on seemed to send chills through his entire body. Although the temperature in the room was purposely frigid, he could feel sweat soaking through his tank top. He could only hope it wouldn't soak through to his uniform before the interview ended.

Dammit, Rocky! I got into this shit to help people, do the right thing. You always have me caught up in some bullshit! I ain't done nothing wrong. Why the hell am I sweating bullets?

"Okay Officer Carrington, let's get started."

Chance sat up straight. "Okay."

Per the lieutenant's request, he methodically relayed the details of the standoff. He would pause periodically to answer questions, but moved through the events leading up to the shooting. When he got to the moment Rocky shot Tim, his stomach twisted in knots. Chance felt nauseous and he could hear the sound of his own heart pounding. This was the moment of truth.

"… As the female was approaching, the suspect suddenly raised and discharged his weapon. Before he could get off another shot, Officer Moretti let off two shots and took him down."

The rest of the questions were a blur. The deception sat in the bottom of Chance's gut like a rock. Satisfied with his answers, the lieutenant ended the interview, escorted Chance to the front of the station where an officer was waiting to drive him back to his workplace.

"Thank you," Chance said while exiting the vehicle. He noticed that Rocky was being dropped off by a different cruiser at the same time. He waved to get Chance's attention, but he pretended not to see him. The last person he wanted to talk to right now is Rocky.

Chance sat on the bench in the locker room. He glanced down at the dried blood droplets that dotted his uniform. Suddenly his collar felt as if it were choking him. He unbuttoned his shirt and rested his face in his hands solemnly. Just as he started to replay the events of the day in his mind, the door to the locker room slammed. Chance looked up just in time to see Rocky coming toward him. It was apparent that his meeting with Lt. Grayson had been unpleasant.

Chance and Rocky had been partners for four years now. Out in the streets, they had naturally settled into the roles of good cop and bad cop. Chance preferred to talk to suspects and victims to resolve matters. Rocky, on the other hand, lived up to his name. He had a reputation of getting physical with suspects and forcing victims to give him the information he needed. He didn't mind getting into a shoot 'em up bang-bang situation when he deemed it necessary. When they first teamed up, Chance had demanded he be reassigned, but Lt. Grayson denied the request. He was well aware of Rocky's past issues and thought that Chance could help to balance him out.

The first couple of months had been rough. The two partners argued over everything from who needed to be arrested to the technique used in questioning witnesses. That all changed on Christmas Eve that year. They had responded to a domestic violence call. The suspect had supposedly fled the scene, but as Chance was interviewing the victim, the man slipped out of a closet and crept up behind him with a baseball bat. Before he was even aware of what had happened, Rocky had shot the perpetrator dead. He had saved Chance's life and from that point on, he would always get the benefit of the doubt when they worked together.

"You ready for another paid vacation?" Rocky asked.

Chance ignored him.

Oblivious to the fact that his partner was seething, Rocky approached and shoved him playfully. "What's your problem, bro?"

Chance leapt off the bench, grabbed Rocky by the collar and slammed him against the lockers.

"What the hell do you think my problem is? I need to be out here working, bro! You had no reason to shoot that man!"

"Shhhhh!" Rocky looked around to be sure no one else was lurking in the locker room. "My line of vision was obstructed. I thought he was aiming his gun. I was just looking out for you."

Chance lowered his gaze and released his grip. This was nothing new. Rocky always shot first and asked questions later. No one in the entire department had discharged their firearm nearly as many times as he had.

"What? You think I fucked up?" Rocky asked.

Chance stammered, "Hell yeah, you fucked up! I just lied about what happened. I could go to jail!"

"I thought he was about to shoot! That's the only reason I shot him." Rocky waited for acknowledgment that his partner and close friend believed him. After receiving no confirmation, he pressed. "Chance, you do believe me, right? As long as we stick to the story, we're good."

"Look, Rocky. It doesn't matter what I believe. You've had my back for four years. You've saved my life. I would never throw you under the bus so you don't have to worry about that."

Rocky breathed a sigh of relief before heading over to his locker to change. Chance sat for a while longer before getting dressed to go home.

Before he left the station, he grabbed a bottle of water from the refrigerator, then retrieved the bottle of Xanax from his duffle bag. He thought about skipping the medication tonight, but wanted to be relaxed when he saw April. He didn't want her worrying about him. He popped a pill into his mouth and washed it down with a swig of water.

April yanked the door open before Chance could insert his key into the lock. He tried not to drop the Thai food he had picked up on his way home when she leaned into him and wrapped her arms around his neck. She pressed her lips hard against his and then began to plant wild, sloppy kisses all over his face.

"If I knew I would be greeted like this, I would have shown up a long time ago," he joked.

"Chance, do not play with me. I was worried about you!" she shrieked.

"You know I'm always safe, April. I will always make it back home to you, baby," he promised.

This time, she kissed him soft and gently, forcing his body to react to her sensuous touch.

"Now, can I come inside and put this food down before I drop it?" he interrupted.

April laughed before releasing her grasp on him and moving aside so he could get by. She plopped down on the couch and continued watching the events of the day unfold on the news. It had been hell getting out of the downtown area with all of the roads blocked off. Luckily, the hostage situation had been resolved right before she was off work. Who knew how long her office would have been on lock down had Chance's team not taken control of the situation.

She glanced in the kitchen and stared at Chance. He was carefully removing the containers of food from the plastic bags and placing them on the counter. He had changed out of his uniform before coming home. She marveled at the fact that he could spend all day chasing down thieves, breaking up domestic violence incidents and showing up for court cases and still look as if he had not broken a sweat. He would even find time to bring something nice home for her each and every evening. She was relieved he had opted for Thai food this week because she was running out of places to put all of the flowers.

"Baby, I'm going to jump in the shower," he advised.

"Okay. Hurry back."

While Chance freshened up, April fixed their plates, poured two glasses of red wine and set them up on the coffee table. He returned to the living room a few minutes later looking relaxed and comfortable in his white t-shirt and boxers. She snuggled up next to him and they ate and watched Friday night television shows together, both grateful for the weekend.

April considered asking him about the incident that had occurred with Rocky during the standoff, but she knew how much he hated to bring his work home. Chance preferred to leave the policing back at the station.

"Babe, wake up!" April ordered.

Chance put the pillow over his head to block out the light that was now beaming through the open blinds. He knew the routine but wasn't feeling up to it.

She snatched the pillow from his face and leaned in, pressing her cheek against his. "Wake up. I'm taking you to breakfast."

"April, I'm not hungry," Chance protested.

"So what? Come anyway," she ordered.

He rolled out of bed moaning and groaning and made his way to the shower. As the steamy streams of water washed over him, he tried his best to shake the anxiety of yesterday but couldn't. April had let him off the hook last night, but today she would want all of the details on the standoff.

The ride to the restaurant was quiet with the radio locked in on the jazz station. Chance knew that April was usually talkative in the car, so the fact that she let the music play for their entire trip let him know that she was in deep thought, likely about their upcoming conversation. He wondered what she had heard. Were the women in her office already discussing it?

7

"So?" April started as soon as the waiter walked away to put in the orders.

"What?" he asked.

She rolled her eyes and moved in closer. "Come on, Chance! You know exactly what. Tell me what happened yesterday."

"I'm sure you've already heard about it, April."

"But I want to hear it from you."

Chance's mouth was suddenly bone dry. He grabbed the glass of water from the table and took a long sip. When he looked up at April, she was staring, awaiting his response. When they had decided to make the relationship official, the agreement was that lying to one another was completely out of the question.

"April, you know I can't talk about this with you. This could become something you have to prosecute."

"This is off the record, Chance. I'm not cross-examining you. I just want to know what happened at work. It's a normal question for a woman to ask her boyfriend." Her voice was high-pitched and sharp. This was not going to be a pleasant meal.

Chance was uncomfortable in his chair. "It is a completely normal question, April. I really want to share everything with you." He picked her hand up from the table and kissed it. "I just want to talk to our union rep and be sure the internal affairs investigation is over first."

April yanked her hand from his and folded her arms across her chest. He leaned back and sighed. Each and every time something happened at work they went through the same song and dance.

"So, my having a casual discussion with you is dependent on the authorization of your union rep, huh?" she snapped.

"Come on, baby. You know damn well there is nothing casual about this conversation. You of all people should understand why I can't discuss it."

April scoffed, but she knew he was absolutely right. It bothered her that they couldn't be vulnerable with one another. Because of their jobs they both kept their guards up around one another and were very careful about what they said.

No longer wanting to argue with him, she conceded. "You wanna catch a movie after breakfast?"

He smiled and nodded, happy to drop the subject.

April hooked her arm through Chance's as they walked toward the box office. She had been wanting to see *The Mountain Between Us* and was happy that they had gotten out early enough to catch a matinee. Now they wouldn't need to worry about a crowded theater. As Chance purchased tickets, April took notice of two couples approaching. When they were close, she recognized the two men as people she had grown up with in South Seattle.

"Tariq and Eric! Oh my God!" she shrieked.

"April! What's up, girl? How you been?" Tarik gave her a tight hug, lifting her off the ground and Eric followed. They both introduced her to their ladies. It has been a long time since she had run into them and it was good to see them free and doing well.

"Hey, you guys see Chance? Babe, come here," she urged as she waved him over.

He took his time turning to face the two men. He wasn't in the mood for this today. Although Chance had not known April as a child, he, too, had grown up with Tariq and Eric. They had all been childhood friends but grown apart as the years went on. Chance had fallen into a career on the police force and his friends had landed on the other side of the law. He had run into them and was forced to make an arrest that resulted in lengthy prison sentences for both of them. After getting out, they had turned their lives around, but had never forgiven him for it. Seeing them was always awkward.

"What's up Tariq? How are you, Eric?" Chance greeted.

Eric grabbed his girl's hand and led her into the theatre dismissing any type of exchange with him. Tariq had always been the outspoken one. There was no way he would ever miss an opportunity to tell Chance exactly how he felt about him.

"What's up, snitch?" he snickered.

"Don't start, Tariq. You know Chance is no snitch!" April interjected.

"April, I don't need you to explain anything to him. If I was a snitch, his ass would still be under the jail. I was just doing my job, but still made sure I looked out for you!" he barked.

"You call two years in the pen for something I didn't do looking out? I'm glad you were doing your job. That must be nice. I couldn't do my job from prison! Do you know what happened to my family while I was locked up?" Tariq stepped closer and pointed in Chance's face.

April moved in front of Tariq in an effort to keep the men separated. *What the hell was I thinking? I should've let these guys keep on walking!*

Chance smirked at Tariq. "Oh, so you're blaming me for your wife leaving you? As if I'm the one who was out here running a drug ring? I tried to look out for your family, but you wouldn't let me."

"You're exactly who I'm blaming! You think you can lock me up and then give my wife and kids some chump change to make up for it?"

The young lady that had arrived with Tariq was slowly moving away, uncomfortable with how passionate he was about the loss of his ex-wife. April felt sorry for her.

"Guys, do you have to act like this whenever you see each other?" she screamed.

Tariq stepped back. "Nah, sis. I ain't got to do anything when it comes to him. He sold out a long time ago. He's the police department's token black dude."

As soon as the words left his lips, Chance was around April and on him. He gripped Tariq's collar with one hand and clenched the other into a fist.

"Chance, stop it!" April grabbed his arm.

He released his grip as if he had suddenly regained his composure and stepped back. Tariq straightened his collar, grabbed his girlfriend by the hand and disappeared into the building.

April walked up behind Chance and rested her hand on his back massaging gently. He jumped at her touch throwing her hand off his back. She stared at him, shocked at his reaction.

"Why are you always bringing that dude over to speak to me?"

"I didn't know—"

"You knew exactly how it was going to go! It's always a problem, April! What I don't get is why their only problem is me. You are a prosecuting attorney, but I'm the only one that's a traitor to my race. You get to still be his sis," he said sarcastically.

"I guess the difference is that I would never prosecute someone I know, Chance." She immediately regretted answering his rhetorical question.

Chance exploded, "Oh, yeah, I forgot. You only want to find a way to prosecute me and the people I work with!"

He turned on his heels and threw the movie tickets in the garbage before stomping to the car. April followed him and settled into the passenger seat for the tense ride home.

FACTS MATTER

April brushed past the line of people waiting to go through the metal detector. The impatient visitors groaned begrudgingly as she greeted the security guard.

"Why the hell is she skipping the line?" a woman whose face had aged far beyond her years squawked.

April spun around, ready to give her a tongue-lashing, but when she looked in the woman's face she just felt sorry for her. Most of her teeth were missing and the ones that remained were reduced to cracked and chipped stubs. As April turned to walk down the hall, the angry lady hurled obscenities in her direction.

Everyone stared as she made her way down the hallway toward the courtroom. April wore a black designer pencil skirt that fit a little more tightly than her mother would have deemed acceptable for work. The *click-clack* of her black leather Louboutin heels drew attention and her red silk blouse laid perfectly against her body. Her jet black curly hair was pulled up into a high bun with a few tendrils hanging down to frame her face. Her lightly applied makeup complimented her honey-colored complexion and her almond-shaped sable eyes.

"Hey, pretty lady!" a man standing with his attorney flirted as she passed him.

April rolled her eyes and sped up her stride. She would never get used to the cat calls she endured every day as she entered the courthouse. *This is not a construction site, asshole!* She thought.

The courtroom was packed and the judge hadn't come in yet.

"Ooh, girl! You look so cute today!" Charlotte mused when April slipped into the seat next to her.

"Thanks, Char. What do we have today?"

Charlotte let out an exasperated sigh. "Girl, same old, same old. Tickets, domestic violence, parole violations. Nothing major."

"Another long, boring day," April surmised. She and Charlotte giggled.

"But tell me about what happened with Chance and Rocky!" Charlotte whispered. "I heard Rocky shot a man while he was giving up!"

April stopped unpacking her briefcase. "I'm sure that's not what happened, Char. Who told you that? That's how rumors get started."

"Well, what did Chance tell you about it?"

April looked down. Charlotte was so judgmental. She could feel her eyes scrutinizing every move she made.

"Oh my God, April. He didn't tell you anything, did he?" Charlotte cried.

"He'll tell me after the investigation is over."

Charlotte narrowed her eyes at April. "Really, April? What kind of relationship is this? He can't even tell you about something major that happened at work?"

April turned and continued unloading her briefcase. This was not the time or the place to get into her and Chance's relationship problems.

Charlotte grabbed her by the shoulders. "Look, April. You and I both know that Rocky should have been out of the department a long time ago... and probably locked up. He's going to go down and he will take Chance with him." She waited for a reply.

ALL RISE! THE HONORABLE JUDGE RON MORRIS PRESIDING!

April was happy for the interruption from the bailiff.

Chance heard the door slam after April walked in. They had barely spoken since the incident at the movies and he was feeling guilty. He hated when work came between them.

April stormed into the room and tossed her purse and briefcase on the coffee table. She stood over Chance ready for confrontation. "So are you going to tell me what happened or not."

He took his feet off of the coffee table sat his beer down. "April, I already told you—"

"Rocky shot someone that was surrendering! How could you not tell me about that, Chance?"

He leaned back and covered his face with his hands. "Let me guess, Charlotte is feeding you this bullshit? You know she can't stand Rocky."

"So, you're telling me it's not true?"

Chance looked away.

April sat next to him and turned his face to her. "Look me in the eye and tell me it's not true, Chance.

He sat silent.

"Are you serious? Are you in trouble?" she asked.

Chance laughed uncomfortably. He hadn't answered her questions, yet she had all of the answers she needed. He couldn't bear to keep it from her any longer anyway.

"Okay, April. Yes, the guy was giving up—at least it looked like he was—and Rocky shot him."

April cupped her hands over her mouth. She knew she should have said something but she was too shocked to utter a single word.

"It's not what you think, April. He didn't have a clear view and didn't know the dude handing his gun over to me. He thought I was going to get shot."

She rolled her eyes. "There's always a logical reason for shooting someone when it comes to Rocky, Chance. Did you tell internal affairs what happened?"

He sat straight up and looked away. He could feel her eyes watching his every move.

April scooted up next to him and placed her hands on either side of his face, forcing him to look at her. "Baby, please tell me you told internal affairs the truth. Tell me you didn't ruin your career for Rocky!"

Chance jerked his head from her hands and leapt to his feet. "What the hell was I supposed to do? He's my partner! He's always had my back!" He paced back and forth frantically.

"What about the man that died… and his wife. Rocky's actions killed her, too!"

"No, April! Rocky didn't hold anybody hostage. He didn't have a standoff with the police! We were there to help and it happened! That man killed his wife and got what he deserved!" Once again, he turned away from her.

April gasped as she brought her hand to her chest. She couldn't believe he was being so callous. She stood and walked over. She wrapped her arms around Chance's shoulders and rested her forehead against his. "I know you, Chance. You care about people. You don't mean what you're saying..."

Chance brought his hands up and placed them on April's hips. His body trembled and tears threatened to run down his face. April hugged him closely. She had only seen Chance cry one time and that was when his mother had died. He tended to tuck his emotions away and keep them buried.

"Baby, I fucked up," he blurted out.

She wanted to tell him that he hadn't messed up and that he had done the right thing. It just wasn't true.

"Chance you can't risk your job and your freedom for Rocky. I won't stand for it."

He backed up and wiped his eyes. "You don't understand, April. I don't just have a job. It's bigger than that," he explained.

"I feel the same way. Both of us want to make an impact and do the right thing, Chance. That's no excuse."

He shook his head back and forth. "I'm not talking about doing the right thing or having a purpose. I'm talking about loyalty and legacy. My dad retired from this department. He made his way through the ranks and finished his career here. He expects me to follow in his footsteps. If I turn on my partner, I will never be promoted. Disloyalty is unacceptable."

"That sounds crazy, Chance."

"It may sound crazy, but it's true. No one expects me to throw Rocky under the bus. The minute I do, they'll do everything they can to get me out of the department because I won't be trustworthy."

April grimaced. What she was hearing turned her stomach. "Well maybe it's time you got out of there."

Chanced threw up his hands. "And go where? You think another department will take me after word gets out that I told on my partner and ruined his life?"

"Maybe you could start an organization and work in our community."

Chance laughed maniacally. "Our community? What community? You still have a community, April! I don't have a community. The moment I became a cop, I became the black sheep. No family... No friends. I'm suddenly a pariah. Even murderers don't get treated like I'm treated by my own people!"

Finally, the elephant in the room had been addressed. When April and Chance had met, she found him irresistible. He was new to the police force and seemed to be popular and social. They were out with friends and family every weekend and everyone seemed to love him. As the years went on, and police shootings of unarmed black men escalated with no justice in sight, Chance started to distance himself from the issues and to everyone outside of the force that knew him, it meant he had taken the side of the police. They couldn't see the moments at home when he punched holes in walls or took his frustrations out on his punching bag because his hands were tied. He felt like a sellout and those closest to him treated him like a stranger. They accused him of being a token black man and the incident that led to Tariq's incarceration cemented his reputation as a traitor and Uncle Tom. April wished everyone else could see what she saw in Chance; a man who cared about his people and his career. He was caught between a rock and a hard place.

April couldn't stand to see him suffer like this. Although her situation was different than his, she could empathize. She was a prosecuting attorney for the State of Washington but she had always considered herself more of a community activist than anything. With a name like April Story, everyone had expected her to follow in her father's footsteps and take up journalism, but she went to law school. She had decided early on in her career that she would focus her efforts on making sure that people who took advantage of others would pay. April never succumbed to pressure from law enforcement or anyone else. She had good instincts and made sure she always did the right thing no matter the consequences. This didn't always put her on the best of terms with Chance's peers. They knew that if a police officer was in the wrong, April would prosecute him to the fullest extent of the law just as she would a common criminal. This had a lot to do with Chance keeping work and home life completely separate.

Chance collapsed face down on the couch, defeated. April slipped out of her heels and laid on top of him, resting her face on the back of his shoulder.

"I get it, Chance. It's not fair. You shouldn't have to choose between your family and friends and your career.

But you're strong, babe. You can find a way to make it work."

He started to roll over and April raised up to let him. Once he was comfortably on his back, she relaxed and top of him with her head on his chest. He ran his fingers through her hair. She always knew the right thing to say to encourage him but would call him out when she didn't agree with his actions. That had been what attracted him to April. Her features were soft and delicate and her petite frame made him want to protect her. But April wasn't the type of girl that needed protection. She commanded both attention and respect when she walked into a room. She was always pleasant; everyone loved her, but if you happened to get on her bad side, you would live to regret it. The contrast of softness and strength turned him on.

He pulled her chin up and kissed her lips. Her eyes closed and her mouth parted beckoning his tongue in. They made out slowly and methodically until he could take it no more. He ripped off her blouse, sending buttons flying every which way and showed her breasts the same attention he had given her lips. They remained on the couch making sweet love until they both drifted to sleep.

Chance walked up behind April as she stood in the mirror combing through the tangled mess of hair atop her head. He wrapped his arms around her waist and nuzzled the back of her neck.

"Mmmmm...," she moaned, loving the warmth of his body on hers. "Chance, what are you doing in here? You should have let me get myself together. I look a mess."

He buried his fingers in her hair and gently pulled her head back, kissing her cheek. "I love when you look like this... no makeup, your hair down. You're beautiful."

April looked herself over in the mirror. Her face was freshly washed and makeup-free. The combination of sweaty love making and the steamy morning shower had transformed her once perfectly put together hair into something between an afro and a twist out. She scrunched her nose up and tilted her head back and forth trying to decide whether or not she needed to flat iron it.

"Wear it like this," Chance said as if reading her mind. He gave her one last peck and exited the bathroom.

April pulled the hem of her long, colorful maxi dress into the car and Chance shut her door. She was feeling Bohemian today with her hair pulled back into a large puffball. The painted wood Ankh Cross Connection earrings she wore bounced around as she and Chance traded light-hearted barbs with one another. His mood had certainly lightened over the last couple of weeks. Internal Affairs had found Rocky's shooting justified and both he and Chance had returned to work. The incident had been buried deep in his psyche along with all of the other skeletons he ignored and the concessions he had to make in consideration of his career. Chance sang along with the music and rocked his head back and forth. He looked over at April, winked and smiled. She could see the tension still present in his tight jaw and wondered how many more secrets his conscience could handle.

"Aye!" April's brother, Michael exclaimed as they pulled up in front of her parent's house.

Her mother and father had moved out to the Tacoma area several years back. The housing prices in Seattle had skyrocketed over the last decade and most of the black people had moved South. They had bought a nice house in the University Place area for half the price it would have cost up north. The neighborhood was quiet and pristine; a perfect place for Mr. and Mrs. Story to retire.

"You ready to play some ball?" Michael asked Chance as he lightly ribbed him.

"Of course. I stay ready. As always, I'm going to run all over y'all!"

April giggled at the two men acting like schoolboys. Every time the family got together, Chance and her brothers would go out into the sprawling backyard and play a game of flag football. The visit gave Chance an opportunity to be around people who did not only associate him with being a police officer. April's family had taken an immediate liking to him as soon as he was introduced; maybe that was due to the fact that Chance had insisted she not disclose his occupation to them right away. She had hated being so vague with her family and by the time she told them that he was a cop, they were relieved. All of the hiding had made Mrs. Story start to wonder if he was a drug dealer or unemployed.

Chance kissed her on the cheek before heading toward the rear of the house to join her father and brothers. April went to the kitchen to help her mother and her sister finish up dinner preparations.

"Hey, baby! How are you?" Mrs. Story asked as she embraced her.

"I'm good, mom." She leaned out and looked at her mother's face. Her smooth olive skin and bright eyes belied her fifty-seven years. Even with her silver hair, she looks at least fifteen years younger than her age.

"Hey, sis!" Janice greeted as she pecked her on the cheek.

Mrs. Story picked up a bunch of collard greens and started removing the stems.

"So, how is Chance holding up?" Janice asked.

Mrs. Story nudged her, wanting her to be quiet.

"It's okay, mom," April said. "He's better now. The investigation is over and the shooting was found to be justified."

"Of course it was!" Janice rolled her eyes.

"Don't start, Jan," Mrs. Story warned.

"I'm just sick of the cops killing us and getting away with it!"

"The guy was white, Janice," April informed.

"And? Does it matter? Somebody is dead that didn't need to be!"

April sighed. "Look, you don't even know the whole story. The guy had a gun!"

Janice leaned in and poked April in the chest as she spoke. "Don't try to sell me that bullshit, sis! Mom already told me what was up!"

April glared at her mother. "Mom, that conversation was between you and I!"

Before Mrs. Story could respond, the men came bustling through the back door.

"Janice, please don't say anything about this to Chance," April pleaded. "I wasn't supposed to tell anyone," she whispered.

Her sister's face softened. "I got you, sis."

Chance, Mr. Story and April's brothers pulled themselves from the Seahawks game and gathered around the table in the dining room as her, Mrs. Story and Janice placed the steaming dishes in the center of the table.

Chance looked around the table at April's family. He had always felt at ease and accepted around them; he wasn't quite sure that would be the case if they knew what kind of things he had done for a paycheck. His gaze froze on Janice. He could've sworn there was a hint of disdain in her eyes as she glared directly at him. She had always been a tough nut to crack. Her position with the Our Lives Count movement had naturally put her at odds with many of his colleagues and he got the idea that she would never fully trust him. Usually they got along but kept one another at arm's length. Today, the tension in her face was palpable and it made Chance shift in his seat. He looked over at April, wondering if she had happened to tell her sister about the situation he'd had at work. She quickly diverted her attention to the conversation taking place at the table and avoided his gaze.

Dinner could not end fast enough. Although the conversation was light-hearted, Janice was like a grey cloud preparing to rain on Chance's parade. He chose a seat as far away from her as possible when they all settled into the family room for drinks.

"So, Chance, I hear you're being considered for Assistant Chief of Police?" Mr. Story asked.

He narrowed his eyes at April. He hated when she told his business before he had an opportunity to share. "Yes, sir. That's right!" he beamed.

Janice scoffed and everyone turned to look at her.

"Everything alright, sis?" Michael asked.

She sipped her drink. "Everything is great! Ain't that right, Chance?"

He furrowed his brow at her and April kicked her lightly in the leg, imploring her to stop.

"What is that supposed to mean?" he barked.

April jumped in. "Babe, you know Jan... always talking mess."

Janice narrowed her eyes at April before dropping the subject and turning away.

Mrs. Story clasped her hands together. "Michael, turn on the 6:00 news for me."

Happy for a reprieve from the evident issues between Janice and Chance, Michael did as his mother asked and flipped between channels looking for the news. He had never understood why his sister held Chance's occupation against him. He couldn't control what every other officer did, so it just didn't make sense.

GOOD EVENING. THIS IS KIRO 7 NEWS. BREAKING TONIGHT, NOT GUILTY! OFFICER JERRY HUGHES HAS BEEN FOUND NOT GUILTY IN THE SHOOTING OF DE'ANDRE WELLS. A JURY HAS FOUND THAT DESPITE THE FACT THAT MR. WELLS WAS UNARMED AND ACTUALLY ENTERING HIS OWN HOME WHEN A NEIGHBOR CALLED 9-1-1 TO

REPORT A BURGLARY, OFFICER HUGHES WAS ACTING IN SELF-DEFENSE WHEN HE GUNNED HIM DOWN IN FRONT OF HIS WIFE AND CHILDREN.

Everyone sat in stunned silence. The De'Andre Wells case had dominated the news cycle for weeks now. Janice had led Our Lives Count in protests at the police station as well as the state capitol in Olympia. Everyone had been so sure that this time would be different; that this time, justice would be served. Mr. Story shook his head back and forth unable to form the words to express how he was feeling. Mrs. Story sat quietly with tears running down her face. She always took these things to heart. Michael just kept saying "damn" over and over for lack of a better word. April closed her eyes to calm her nerves. When the State set the prosecution of Officer Hughes in motion they had all been certain that the case was a slam dunk. Everything was there; documented racism, eyewitnesses, scientific evidence and a history of brutality. She clenched her fists against the arms of the chair. Chance swallowed hard. He, too, had hoped the officer would be found guilty. Then he could finally prove to everyone that the law actually worked. But, of course, once again, he would find himself in the position of defending the indefensible.

"This is bullshit!" Janice yelled. She slammed her glass down on the coffee table, stood up and stormed out of the room. April ran after her.

"I'm so sorry," Chance offered to everyone left in the room.

"Don't take Janice's actions personal, bro. You're not responsible for every other cop's actions," Michael assured him. He patted Chance on the shoulder.

"Jan, I understand you being upset, but taking it out on Chance and disrespecting him is not acceptable," April said as she slipped into the seat on the patio.

Janice was pacing back and forth. She stopped and looked at April dumbfounded. "What do you mean, April? You know exactly what my problem is with Chance! I'm just surprised that you are putting up with it."

"Putting up with what?" she rolled her eyes.

"You can't be out here fighting for people's rights and going after the bad guys but overlooking the snake in your own house!"

"Snake? That's drastic, Janice. Chance is not a snake!"

Janice laughed. "Well, at the very least he's weak as hell. If he is really a good guy amongst a bunch of bad ones, it's worse than I thought. You've never liked weak men, April."

April's looked down at the ground. She knew her sister was right. "He really is a good dude. It's like years of dealing with these things just took the fight out of him. You don't understand what it's like trying to survive in the world of law enforcement as a black man."

"That's B.S. and you know it!" She was pacing again. "You graduated at the top of your class with a law degree. You could make as much money as you want, doing anything you want, but you do what's right! How can you be the strongest person in your relationship? Your man is supposed to lead!"

April leapt from her seat and got close to Janice. "You have no idea what kind of man Chance is or what he's been through! Don't you dare insinuate that he's weak because there are not a lot of men that could have gone through everything he has and still been standing!" Janice backed up, but April inched closer, still upset. "You can't put your assumptions aside long enough to be unbiased. Do not disrespect him again!"

Janice threw her hands up in surrender, turned on her heels and rushed back into the house.

She and her sister had always been the best of friends and rarely had a disagreement; at least before Chance came around. They had both gotten involved in community activism as teens and typically thought along the same lines when it came to social matters. Never in a thousand years had Janice imagined her sister would get romantically involved with one of the very people they sat out to protect the community from.

Janice blew past Chance on her way out the front door. He was glad she had ignored him on her way out.

Michael shook his head. His sister was very upset by the outcome of the trial and rightfully so, but he could not understand why on earth she took it out on Chance. He wasn't even in the same department as the accused officer.

April looked at Chance as she walked in. His head was bowed and his shoulders slumped. She couldn't blame him for avoiding these discussions. Somehow he always turned out to be responsible for the actions of every other member of law enforcement. On the flip side, at work they expected him to answer for the actions of every other black person in America. He couldn't defend the police when they were right about something unless he wanted to be looked at as a sellout. He was unable to confront his colleagues or voice his opinion when he knew them to be wrong or he would be looked at with suspicion and could kiss any chance of getting that promotion goodbye.

April knelt in front of him and softly caressed his face with the back of her hand. "Are you alright?" she asked.

"I'm good," he blurted. Chance was not one to let his emotions get the best of him.

"I'm sorry that happened. Janice just gets so emotional about these things."

"I don't blame her for getting emotional," he replied. "It's fucked up! There should have been a guilty verdict. But I'm upset, too! It's not like I was rooting for him to get off!"

"I know, babe. I know." April wrapped her arms around his neck and held him tight.

"Baby, why don't you take Chance home? Y'all relax and get some rest." Mrs. Story winked at Chance and his shoulders relaxed.

"You're absolutely right, Mrs. Story," he agreed. He kissed her on the cheek, shook Mr. Story's hand and grabbed April's coat.

As April slipped into her coat she scanned Chance's face, unable to read his mood. The situation with Janice was getting old. It wasn't fair that he had to take the brunt of her frustration. After buttoning up, she grabbed his hand and led him toward the car.

LITTLE BOY LOST

The phone rang, startling Chance as he read over the article for the fifth time.

"Hi, Dad," he greeted. He sat straight up in his chair. Mr. Carrington was always on him about his posture as a child.

"Good evening, son. How goes it?"

Chance grimaced. He hated beating around the bush.

"Everything is great. I'm still waiting on the promotion if that's what you're asking about," he snapped.

Mr. Carrington's voice boomed through the phone. "I was actually checking to see how my only son is doing. Don't take that tone with me."

Chance started to speak but kept his mouth shut.

"Hello? Do you hear me, boy?"

"Yes, sir," Chance finally mumbled.

Switching right back to his upbeat tone, Mr. Carrington continued, "So, word is that you held your own when you were questioned about the shooting. I'm proud of you, son."

Chance's stomach turned and bile rose in his throat. "Watching a life taken and lying about it is nothing to be proud of."

"Of course it is! Don't be naive, Chance. Yes, you are there to help people when you can, but you are part of a team and your job is to protect the team."

"No. My job is to serve and protect the public. My *job* is to make my community better!"

Mr. Carrington roared with laughter. "Forget about them thugs in your so-called community. The department has been good to us. We have done well. You are there to carry on my legacy and if you mess this up, you and I are done."

Chance's heart raced and a lump formed in his throat. Memories of himself as an eight-year-old boy popped into his head. His dad was packing his belongings while he and his mother begged him not to go. Oblivious to their pain, he had seemed almost gleeful as he looked back at his son one last time before slamming the door behind him. Chance had raced to the front window to catch one last glimpse of his father and saw him getting into the car with a woman with long, blonde hair and piercing blue eyes. She had to be half his age and wore a smirk on her thin red lips. Mrs. Carrington almost collapsed when she ran outside and witnessed the reason for her husband's sudden departure. His passenger seemed to revel in her despair as they sped off into the sunset.

Chance cleared his throat. "I gotta go. I'll talk to you later." Before his father could object, he hit the end button.

He glanced at the picture of the exonerated officer smiling for the cameras one last time before slamming his laptop shut. His clenched fists slammed down on either side of the solid oak desk with a loud hollow thud.

April burst into the room with a hot pink oven mitt on her hand and a matching apron tied around her waist. "Are you okay?"

Chance feigned a smile. "I'm good, baby."

She raised her eyebrow. "You sure you don't want to talk about it?"

"There's nothing to talk about. I'm good." He walked over and kissed her lips. "I'm going to head out into the garage and workout."

April smiled at him before returning to the kitchen.

Sweat soaked Chance's white tank top and his sculpted biceps flexed over and over as he pounded the punching bag. DMX's *Ruff Ryder's Anthem* blasted through the Bluetooth speaker. Chance's brow furrowed and the longer the song went on the harder he hit the bag. He replayed his conversation with his father and swung until the memory vanished. Next thoughts of Tariq invaded his mind. Back in the day they had been tight and had bonded over their absent fathers. Tariq's dad was doing a lifelong bid in Clallam Bay Correctional Center and had been there for as long as he could remember.

Chance's father wasn't locked up but may as well have been. He had remarried, started a new family, and all but forgotten about his ex-wife and son. Chance had always been athletic and excelled in every sport he played. He remembered inviting Mr. Carrington to his basketball and football games, only to be disappointed when he didn't show. He believed that he was paying enough in child support to not be pestered about his parenting or the lack thereof. He finally took notice when Chance decided to join the police academy. Suddenly, he was visiting on a regular basis, giving advice and setting expectations. At first it was exciting to finally have his father in his life. Once the realization set in that Mr. Carrington's interest wasn't selfless, it became irritating. Still, Chance could not bear to lose his father again.

When Chance met him, Tariq was street savvy, tough and mature for his age. He had accepted his dad's departure long ago. He helped Chance to become the man of his house and take care of his mother. Tariq had taught him how to fight, making him the second toughest kid in the neighborhood. He also encouraged him to get into sports, which led to him dominating on the court and the field.

Chance's mother had passed away when he was sixteen and Tariq's mom had taken him in until he was old enough to take care of himself. They had been the only family he knew. Even after joining the force, he had looked out for his best friend and even overlooked some things that may have been outside of the law. That fateful day when Chance was riding with Rocky in the south end had been one of the worst days of his life. Tariq and Eric were pulled over for a broken tail light. Rocky wanted to search the car but Chance told him not to. He was certain that nothing that had taken place during the traffic stop had risen to probable cause. Rocky persisted anyway and found a couple of pounds of marijuana in the trunk. Both men were arrested and subsequently sentenced to prison. Tariq and Eric had lodged illegal search and seizure and misconduct complaints against the department, claiming that Rocky had lied in the police report; they claimed he had actually planted drugs in the car. In the aftermath, Chance had been questioned about the arrest. His sergeant had warned that if he sided with his friends, his career was over. In the end, he decided to claim ignorance and any opportunity at a successful appeal was lost. That brought a screeching halt to the brotherhood that Chance had once shared with Tariq. Not only had Chance lost his closest friend, he forfeited the only family he had known.

He once again pushed the painful thoughts out of his mind and pummeled the bag a while longer before heading over to the weight set. He piled the bar with more heavy metal plates than he had ever lifted. When his back pressed against the cold leather bench, he began pressing the heavy bar up and down until the muscles in his arm felt as though they would give out. When he could lift no more, he placed the weighted bar back on its rack and laid on his back on the bench. Chance pulled his phone out of his pocket and scrolled to Tariq's number. He stared at it for a while before flinging the phone into the concrete wall, shattering it. He added more plates to the bar and got set to lift again.

April walked into the garage and Chance lifted his head to look at her, still laying on the bench. He immediately took notice of her recent wardrobe change. She had removed the dusty apron she cooked in to reveal a see-through, sleeveless floor-length gown with nothing but a thong on beneath. She walked over to the weight bench and straddled him, immediately taking the weight of the world off his shoulders.

Janice slipped out of the door and made sure it closed behind her. She grabbed April by the arm, yanking her in the opposite direction. Once they were out in the lobby of the building, she stopped and folded her arms across her chest.

"April, what are you doing here?" she asked.

"What kind of welcome is that?" she joked.

Janice shifted to her other foot and furrowed her eyebrows.

"Okay! I just wanted to talk to you." she explained.

Janice wrinkled her forehead. "And you couldn't have picked a better time than now to talk?"

April grinned. "Well, I kind of wanted to come down and see what this was all about."

Janice tried to maintain her irritable stance, but the giddy look on her sister's face made her smile.

"You sure your little boyfriend would approve of you coming down here to be among us common folk?" she teased with a twang in her voice.

April punched her in her arm lightly.

"It's not like that. Chance actually agrees with what the movement is all about."

Janice chuckled. "Really? Then why is it that he never seems to stand up to his buddies?"

"How do you know what he does or doesn't do? You are making assumptions that aren't true! Give him a break, Jan!"

Janice's face softened. She spread her arms to embrace her sister. "You must really be feeling him." They both laughed. "So what's up?"

"I really did want to come to a meeting. I need to be around some people that can relate to how I'm feeling right now," April admitted.

Janice tilted her head to the side and gave her sister the once over. April's posture was perfect; her head held high and a look of strength and confidence pasted on her face. But there was no one closer to her than Janice. She could see past the stoic exterior. The faint hints of doubt and longing in April's eyes told her that everything on the home front wasn't as good as it appeared and the she might be needed right now.

"Okay, sis," Janice started. "You can come in with me, but please just stay quiet and try to blend in," She looked April up and down and knew there was no chance of her blending in with the casual crowd. "And whatever you do, please don't start telling folks you're a prosecutor or that you live with a cop!"

April rolled her eyes. "Okay! I know how to act, Janice. I'm not a child!"

She once again felt her little sister's eyes wandered over her and suddenly felt self-conscious.

"Humph..." Janice grunted before turning around and motioning for April to follow her.

As they approached the door, April paused to slip out of her blazer. She untucked her sleeveless blouse from her skirt and unbuttoned the top button. Next she yanked her hair tie off, dismantling the perfect bun she had worn all day.

"You done or do you need a moment?" Janice quipped as she watched her with her arms folded across her chest.

April blushed. "Shut up. I'm ready."

Janice opened the door and the poetic sound of Iyana James, a well-known community activist's voice floated out of the speakers, filling the room with her powerful melody.

As the woman spoke about police brutality in the community, the crowd chanted. Her controlled yet emotional tone seemed to capture everyone in the room, telling them exactly when to speak and what to say. April found herself staring at the woman in amazement. The dashiki she wore was multicolored and her locks had been pulled back and tied up at her neck. Small seashells danced on the ends of them as she swayed her head back and forth to the rhythm of her own voice. When she finished her speech the entire room rose and applauded. She nodded humbly before taking her seat near the side of the stage.

"On my God! She was so powerful!" April turned to Janice and exclaimed.

Janice nodded in amusement. "She really was! But you ain't seen nothing yet, sis!" With that, she turned April back around to face the stage.

There was an air of anticipation in the air as every woman and man awaited the next speaker. April looked around and took note at the expressions of excitement on their faces. It was clear that although Iyana James had been amazing, she wasn't the person that had drawn the crowd. Even Janice clasped her hands together and rocked back and forth. The man at the podium hushed the crowd.

"And now the moment you've all been waiting for... Dr. Rahim Salek!"

April stood on her toes to see over the cheering audience. Out of the shadows walked the man of the hour. He stood about six feet tall and his build was muscular but slender. He was dressed comfortable in a fitted t-shirt, loose fitting jeans and his stride was long and confident as he approached the podium. His hair was freshly cut; his beard and mustache perfectly lined. His smooth ebony skin glowed, even under the dim lights. He smiled as he greeted the host and each of his cheeks flaunted a boyish dimple. When he finally took his place at the front of the room, he adjusted his gold-rimmed glasses and licked his lips before he spoke. The small gesture seemed to make every woman in the room uncomfortable as they shifted positions. April laughed to herself, certain that the good doctor knew exactly what kind of affect his actions would have.

Let's hear what this pretty boy has to say, April thought.

He cleared his throat. When he finally spoke, she was taken aback by his deep voice. "They want us to accept the murder of our brothers by the police. They want us to go on with our lives and just be happy it wasn't us this time. But we know better than that! When one of us is treated unjustly, all of us are!"

The crowd cheered and nodded in agreement.

He continued. "We will not back down! We will not go away! We will be heard! Our Lives Count!"

The crowd started chanting repeatedly, "Our Lives Count! Our Lives Matter! Our Lives Count!" April and Janice joined in.

The doctor laid out a plan of action for the next few months. There would be petitions, meetings with lawmakers and protests. April was astonished by the level of detail and organization. She had always assumed that these protests just popped up and were motivated by emotion and grief. To see that they were planned and based on real goals made her stand at attention. Near the end of the doctor's speech, he invited the widows and children of unarmed men recently killed by the police and the room was somber. There was not a dry eye as each family member explained how the loss of their loved one had affected them. Finally, there was a group prayer and the meeting concluded.

Janice dragged April around from person to person, introducing her, but was sure to leave out her profession. It was odd because April had always prided herself in her accomplishments as a prosecuting attorney. To meet people and not be able to use that as her crutch made her self-conscious.

Finally, the doctor approached. He first thanked Janice for organizing the event and briefly checked to make sure the next meeting was set up.

"Oh, by the way, this is my sister, April."

April extended her hand to shake his. "Hello, Dr. Salek. It's very nice to meet you."

He took her hand and cupped his other hand over it. "Please, call me Rahim. It's a pleasure to meet you as well, counselor."

She froze, unsure how to respond. She glared at Janice.

"I recognize you from the news," he explained. "From what I hear, you are the best prosecuting attorney in the country."

"Um... I guess that's a matter of opinion," she stuttered.

Rahim pursed his lips. "Don't be modest, Ms. April. You are good at what you do and I'm happy you decided to join us," his piercing opal eyes staring at her intensely.

April turned away and nodded. When she pulled her hand from his, she could still feel the warmth permeating her skin. They all stood silent for several awkward moments before Janice spoke.

"Well, then, I guess I will see you on the next one, Rahim."

"Sounds good. I hope your beautiful sister will join us again." He smiled, once again flashing his deep dimples.

April rolled her eyes. *This guy's good.*

"Of course she will join us again," Janice answered as she nudged her.

"Good. I will be looking forward to it." Once again, he stared directly into April's eyes causing her to divert her attention elsewhere.

With that, Janice prodded April toward the door. Rahim watched until the women were out of sight.

"Well, damn, he sure was checking for you hard!" Janice giggled.

April sighed. "He was just being polite."

Her sister flashed a sarcastic glance.

"And even if that's true, I am not at all interested. I have a man."

Janice scrunched her face up but didn't say a word.

April could hear the soft sounds of Freddie Jackson playing from the front porch. She peeped in the window and saw Chance dancing as he put the finishing touches on dinner while crooning, *"You are my lady... you're all I'm living for."*

She opened the front door and stepped inside. The smell of seafood, butter and garlic sauce and sautéed vegetables wafted through the air and he stomach rumbled. Chance rushed over, scooped her up into his arms and spun her around. April placed her hands on his shoulders and pushed herself back, puzzled by his current state. Chance gently placed her feet back on solid ground, took her hand and pulled her over to the couch.

"Chance, what is going on?" she asked, searching his face for answers.

He could barely sit still as he delivered the news. "I'm one of the finalists for Assistant Chief of Police!"

She dropped her jaw, stunned. "What? How? When?"

Chance laughed. "I was just called into the lieutenant's office and he let me know that he would be submitting my name."

April's expression dropped. "In exchange for what?"

"That's the thing, baby. I don't have to do a thing. He's grateful for how I handled myself in the recent situation and thinks I deserve to be in the top spot." He glanced down bashfully.

April rolled her eyes. "So he's doing this to reward you for lying about a shooting? Chance, you can't accept this."

He clasped his hands together and looked into her eyes. "I know, April. What I did wasn't right. But if I get into this position, I can reform the department and make a real difference. I'm limited as an officer, but as Assistant Chief, I will have real power!"

She had always been a sucker for an activist and right now Chance was starting to sound as if he'd had this plan all along.

"Chance, are you telling me that once you get this job, things will change?"

He stopped and grabbed her by the shoulders. "That's exactly what I'm saying. I can change policies, and make sure that nobody who kills, including cops, goes unpunished!"

April's eyes filled with tears. Lately Chance had been beaten down by the conflicts between his job and his family and friends. It seemed he had finally found a way to do his job while standing by his morals and beliefs. She wrapped her arms around his neck and held him for a while.

"You wanna know what will be the most satisfying, April?" he whispered into her ear. Not waiting for a response, he continued, "I will go further than my dad ever did. He will never have the right to look down on me again."

She held him tighter and he reciprocated. April hated what his father had done to him.

Chance walked through the station with his shoulders back and his chin high. Word had gotten around that he was being considered for the top spot. Every one of his colleagues he walked past gave him a handshake or a pat on the back. If he'd had any doubt that lying about Rocky's shooting, this assured him that he had made the right decision.

Chance stepped into the locker room and started to change into his uniform. The locker next to him slammed and he noticed Rocky standing there.

"Hey, what's up, Roc?" he greeted.

Rocky stared at Chance menacingly before throwing his bag over his shoulder and heading toward the door.

Chance scratched his head as his partner walked away. He and Rocky had barely spoken since the shooting incident. Now that they were both back off administrative leave, Chance was ready to put the entire situation behind him. He waved Rocky off and continued to get dressed.

Once he had finished changing, Chance walked through the station and out the front door, expecting Rocky to be waiting in the squad car. He looked around, unable to locate him in the parking lot. Finally, frustrated, he stalked back into the station and ducked into the lieutenant's office.

"Hey, you seen Rocky?"

The captain stopped writing and waved Chance into his office. His body language seemed to indicate that he needed to shut the door behind him.

"What's up, Lt. Grayson? Is everything good?" he asked.

"Have a seat, Carrington," he motioned toward the empty chair.

Chance sat down and waited to hear what he had to say.

"Moretti asked that he be assigned a new partner."

Chance frowned, thrown off by the assertion. "Why?" He and Rocky had their share of disagreements over the years, but he could think of nothing he had done to make him no longer want to work with him.

Lt. Grayson stared at him. "Listen, son. You've done nothing wrong. You are exactly what this department needs. You're loyal and have always been upfront with me. I am certain that you are going places."

Chance nodded, still not understanding what this had to do with his friend.

The captain continued. "Sometimes in life, it's necessary to drop dead weight in order to excel. You've looked out for Moretti on numerous occasions. You've been a good friend and exemplary partner. It's time to move on."

Chance nodded.

"I have put my name and your father's name on the line by recommending you for the promotion and we can't allow a loose cannon to mess things up. For the rest of your tenure on patrol, you're flying solo."

Again, Chance nodded before shaking Lt. Grayson's hand and leaving. His mind was spinning. He had worked side-by-side with Rocky his entire career as an officer. This would be his first time riding out alone and it felt awkward.

The new patrol car felt unfamiliar. Gone was the outdated Crown Victoria. Chance had received a brand new Chevy Mustang to drive. Cruising down Martin Luther King, Jr. Way felt strangely unfamiliar. He had grown up on these streets and spent his entire adult life here. Yet he suddenly felt like a baby without a security blanket.

Chance had worked so hard for this. He had bitten his tongue repeatedly and neglected to stand up for what he believed in just to make it to this point. He would finally have the opportunity to prove to his father that he was good enough; and to his community that he was not an "Uncle Tom". He was a man with a plan, patience and strategy who knew how to act in order to get what he wanted.

The radio suddenly came to life as the dispatcher read off the address of an ongoing disturbance. Another protest had gotten out of control. With the most recent officer acquittal on police brutality charges, activists and citizens across the city were showing up and disrupting things more frequently. Chance turned on his lights and sirens before pressing the gas pedal to the floor to get there.

When he pulled up to the South Precinct, he couldn't believe how many people had crowded the street in front. Traffic had come to a standstill and officers were attempting to herd everyone to the sidewalks. The angry people had no intentions of following orders. The waved their signs in the air, shouting, "No Justice, No Peace, No Criminal Police!" repeatedly. As Chance pulled his cruiser to the shoulder, he sighed before exiting the vehicle. He could certainly understand the frustration. Officer Hughes had murdered the young man in cold blood. He deserved to be in prison right now. Instead, he had an entire year of paid administrative leave, only to be found not guilty and return to his position. Despite his personal views, Chance had a job to do. He weaved through the crowd, gently nudging the protesters out of his way. He ignored the name-calling, jeers and hateful glares as he pressed on. Chance had heard it all before, but could never get used to being reviled by people that looked like him.

Finally making it to the front of the crowd, he stopped and looked at the man who commanded everyone's attention, Dr. Rahim Salek. Chance knew exactly who he was; everyone knew exactly who he was. He would speak on behalf of victims and their families. He would get in the Police Chief's face and ask the tough questions and any time he deemed it necessary, he would show up with thousands of his supporters, ready to take on law enforcement.

Rahim's voice swept over the crowd, first soothing them and next riling them up. They held onto his every eloquent word, their emotions ebbing and flowing at his command. Chance had to admit that the brother had a way about him that drew people in. He felt a tinge of jealousy at the way everyone responded to Rahim. He had never been the smooth type.

They had come into contact on multiple occasions due to their respective lines of work. Rahim was guaranteed to be first on the scene after an injustice had taken place and Chance just happened to be the lead officer negotiating the dispersing of the crowd. As he walked up, Rahim passed his mic to one of his partners who immediately picked up where he left off inciting the crowd. He walked over and extended his hand. Chance took it and gave him a firm shake.

"What's up, Officer Carrington?" Rahim started.

"You know what's up, doc. Your people are blocking traffic. Not only that, the officers can't get in and out of the precinct. I need you to tell them to leave."

Rahim chuckled. "My people, huh? I thought these were your people, too, brother."

Chance shifted his weight. "Listen, I am not going to do that with you today. I'm just here to do my job. That's all. Don't make it hard on me."

The man stared at him for several seconds and Chance felt uncomfortable under his judgmental eyes. By this time, the crowd had quieted and was listening to the interaction between the men.

"How degrading it must be to just be here to do your job... for your master-- I mean boss... to have no empathy or concern for the struggles of your community. I'm going to pray for you, brother. I'm going to pray for your freedom of thought and expression. I'm going to pray that one day, you have the strength and mental fortitude to be a man."

Amens erupted throughout the crowd. Chance was livid. He could feel his body tensing up.

"Just ask these people to leave before somebody gets hurt." He looked into Rahim's eyes to let him know he meant business.

Rahim scoffed before turning around and waving his hand in the air. As if under a spell, the crowd began to walk away silently. He gave Chance one last up and down before turning on his heels and leaving.

"Don't worry about anything that race baiter has to say." Rocky appeared by his side and placed one hand on his shoulder. Chance had told him about the struggles of a black cop working in the black community and he got it.

Without a word, he returned to his cruiser and drove off.

April heard Chance pull into the driveway and was excited. She couldn't wait to hear about his day. Ever since he had told her about his plans to move up in the department and change the way police interacted with the local community, she felt more connected to him. April has always been a sucker for an activist and the thought of Chance strategically working his way through the system and making it to the top in order to help his people really turned her on. She looked down at the black lace baby doll dress she was wearing. It left nothing to the imagination and she was certain Chance would not be able to control his reaction.

The key turned in the lock and April quickly settled on the couch with her best "come hither" look on her face. Chance walked in and placed his keys, badge and gun on the table in the entryway. He barely noticed her, but muttered an inaudible greeting as he passed by headed to the bedroom. April scoffed and jumped up from the couch, following closely.

"Uh... Hello?" she said.

Chance continued to unbutton his shirt, oblivious to April's irritation. She walked over and stood in front of him.

"So you're just going to ignore me? What's going on, Chance?"

"Oh, hey, baby," he greeted as if this was the first time he noticed her. He looked her up and down and ran his tongue over his lips. "You look tasty."

April looked down at herself, remembering that she was half-naked. No longer in the mood, she folded her arms across her chest.

"Thanks, Chance. But what's going on with you? You were preoccupied when you walked in."

He feigned a smile. "I'm good. Just a long day at work," he replied. Chance was not in the mood to talk about it and hoped she wouldn't press.

True to form, April did not fall for his nonchalant dismissal. "Tell me what happened."

Chance sighed as he discarded his shirt. It was no use trying to minimize what he was feeling. April knew him too well.

"I did the protest in front of the South Precinct today."

"By Our Lives Count?"

"Yep, that's the one." Chance's mouth formed into a sarcastic smile.

April's heartbeat sped up. She met a lot of the people in the group at the meeting she had attended and hoped nothing bad had happened to any of them.

"Their protests are usually pretty peaceful. Was there a problem?"

"It was cool. I mean the people were calm, so that wasn't the issue." Chance answered.

"Okay. So what happened?"

He shifted in his seat before continuing. "So I was in charge of getting the crowd to move on because…"

"Because you're the black cop?" April finished.

He nodded. She shook her head back and forth.

"Anyway, I had to walk up to the leader, this pompous asshole who calls himself Dr. Rahim Salek…" Chance made air quotes as he said the name.

April sat quietly. When she had me Dr. Salek, he put out an air of extreme confidence and knowledge, but never came off as pompous.

"I had to walk up on him in front of the crowd of people… black people and ask him to disperse the crowd."

"Okay." April prodded him on.

"So I ask him to tell his people to move 'cause they were blocking traffic and he starts talking about how I'm supposed to be one of his people to, basically calling me a traitor and telling me to report to my master!"

April was taken aback. Dr. Salek seemed to have an extensive vocabulary and did not seem like the type of man that would resort to name calling. "He actually used that word? He called you that?"

Chance huffed. "No, April. He didn't say the word traitor. That part was more implied. He basically said that it must be degrading to be the token black guy sent to calm down the black people. He insinuated that I am being used."

April raised her eyebrows.

"I see. You think I'm being used, too?" He stood up and began pacing back and forth.

"I mean, you and I know they send you out to deal with problems in the black community. We know that and we deal with it because you are working toward the bigger picture."

"Ugh!" Chance swept his hand across the dresser, knocking everything that was on top to the floor.

April startled. She didn't know what the words were to help him feel better.

"I have to put my feelings aside every day for a damn paycheck! I go out here and risk my life, while saving other people's lives. This dude just dresses nice and speaks well and everyone respects him!" he fumed.

They both knew that what he was saying wasn't true. Rahim had grown up in the hood with a single parent mother. After a stint in juvenile detention, he had pulled himself up by his bootstraps and finished high school at the top of his class. He went on to get double Master's degrees in Psychology and African American Studies while simultaneously becoming the face of the Our Lives Count Movement. He was always on the front lines when there was an injustice in the black community, even getting himself arrested and assaulted by the police in the process. His organization had started a criminal defense fund that freed over one hundred wrongfully convicted men and successfully beat frivolous charges routinely. Our Lives Count also ran a few homeless shelters, a food bank and helped with social issues for those in need. Dr. Salek's resume was beyond impressive.

I guess now is a terrible time to tell him about the meeting I attended, April mused.

Chance stormed into the bathroom and slammed the door. April could hear the shower turn on and she listened as the sound of the water running attempted to drown out his muffled sobs. She promised herself that she would do whatever it took to help Chance with the situation.

"Sis, turn on the news... Channel 5," Janice blurted out before April could even say hello.

April rushed over and grabbed the remote control with one hand while attempting to pin her hair up with the other. She flipped to Channel 5 just as footage of Dr. Salek was playing. She had to admit, the camera loved him. He looked almost as good on television as he did in person. Even the newscaster marveled at his chiseled good looks and his powerful voice.

"This is from the protest at the station yesterday," April mused.

Before Janice could respond, Chance came into the frame and walked up to the doctor. With the microphone still in place, the conversation was clear. He asked Rahim to disperse the crowd. Rahim calmly shot back, telling Chance that these were his people out here protesting. April cringed because Chance immediately lost his cool and came off as a corny cop trying to play the tough guy. The doctor, still as calm as ever, proceeded to embarrass Chance in front of the whole crowd. April wanted to go back in time and erase the whole incident. He had to be utterly humiliated.

"Hahahahaha! I guess he got him told!" Janice screeched into to phone.

"That is not funny, Janice! He didn't have to do him like that!"

"April, please! You know Chance brought that on himself; trying to show his damn colleagues that he was tough and had *the blacks* under control."

"He doesn't think like that, Janice. You have the wrong idea about him. He's just trying to make it to the top so he can affect real change."

Janice laughed uncontrollably. "Yeah, I'm sure I have it all wrong. Like the time he pretended not to know me and my friends because he was with his white co-workers? Or the time he let his best friend get arrested--"

"Okay! That's enough! He is trying to find a way to do right by his people without risking his career. It's not easy, but he's figuring it out."

"If you say so... "Janice mocked.

"I gotta go," April said and hung up without awaiting her sister's reply.

PICK A SIDE

The air in the courtroom was so thick, you could cut it with a knife. Behind counsel for the defense sat most of Seattle's finest. All eyes focused on April as she made her way to the prosecution table with her client right on her heels. The officers whispered to one another and glared at her disgustedly. She was unbothered. This wasn't April's first rodeo. In the seven years she had practiced law, she had successfully tried twenty-three police brutality cases.

"Lieutenant..." She greeted as she passed Chance's boss, seated in the front row with his subordinates.

The Captain shot her a hateful glance and turned his attention back to the front of the courtroom.

"This is going to be a lot of fun," her client whispered nervously into her ear as they sat down.

"Relax, Robert. We are in an ideal position. Don't be intimidated. I got this," she reassured as she looked him squarely in the eyes and gave his shaking hand a squeeze.

"But the whole freaking department showed up!" he said as he gestured toward the gallery across the aisle.

April leaned in closer. "Robert, you have a lot of support, too!" she motioned behind her. "You need to be confident. Do not let them see you sweat."

The both turned to look at the supporters who had crammed into the courtroom to witness justice. A smile slowly spread across his face as the crowd offered words of support. They erupted into a chant, yelling "JUSTICE FOR ROBERT!" over and over.

April's eyes locked on a figure in the crowd. It didn't matter if there were a million people in the room, Rahim Salek would stand out. He stood stoic in the back of the room against the wall with his hands clasped together in front of him. His black button up shirt was fresh-pressed, but untucked and hung loosely over the top of a pair of Tom Ford jeans, perfectly tailored to fit. His signature gold-rimmed spectacles sat on the bridge of his nose. His fade was crisp and his line-up was flawless. He locked eyes with April and flashed his ivory teeth, revealing a dimple in his right cheek. He nodded, acknowledging her. April smiled slightly and diverted her attention back to the front of the courtroom. She could feel perspiration starting to dampen her undershirt.

"Order in the court!" the judge yelled, quieting the crowd as he banged his gavel.

The room was so quiet; you could hear a pin drop as the jury filed in.

"Foreman, have you all reached a verdict?" the judge asked.

"We have, your honor," he replied.

As the bailiff retrieved the paper, April could hear Robert's labored breathing next to her. She took his hand and it was dripping wet with sweat. She sucked in a deep breath as she braced herself for the outcome.

Once the verdict was passed back to the foreman, he began to read. "We the jury find the defendant, Officer

Kenneth Russo guilty of attempted murder in the second degree."

The entire courtroom let out a collective gasp. Robert's supporters began hugging one another and crying tears of joy. The police officers in attendance sat in stone-faced disbelief. Officer Russo's wife and children burst into tears and had to be held up by everyone around them to keep from fainting. The officer attempted to comfort his family, but the bailiff cut him off and took him into custody. April couldn't help but feel sorry for his family. There would be no winners in this situation.

"You should have died!" he screamed as he tried to fight his way to Robert. His colleagues and his attorney did their best to calm him down, but he had to be dragged away kicking and screaming. His supporters solemnly filed out of the courtroom.

Robert hugged April tight. "Thank you so much for getting me through this. Thank you." His eyes welled with tears.

"You're welcome, sir. I'm glad justice was served."

He ran over to his family and friends and they gleefully embraced him. April watched as they all exited. She opened her briefcase and began shoving the case files in. She breathed a long, deep sigh of relief. She couldn't wait to see Chance this evening and fill him in on the details.

"Good morning, Ms. Story."

April was startled and swung around to see who was addressing her.

"Oh my God! I thought I was the only one left in here. You scared the heck out of me, Dr. Salek!"

"My apologies, counselor," he replied, giving her a courtesy bow.

April smiled, amused by his chivalry. "I am very surprised to see you here."

"Why is that?" he asked.

She narrowed her eyes at him. "Robert just doesn't seem like someone you would represent."

Rahim chuckled. "Because he's white?"

"Well... yeah. I thought your mission was to fight for the rights of underserved demographics." she teased.

"You are absolutely right. That is my mission. What exactly do you believe is an underserved demographic?"

"Minorities, LGBTQ, immigrants, women, people with disabilities..."

He laughed.

April folded her arms across her chest. "You disagree?"

"I don't. I just think there are more than that."

"Such as?"

"For your client specifically, his demographic is the poor. Not only are black people being mistreated by the police. The poor are in the same boat, albeit to a lesser extent," he explained.

"That makes sense. I just thought you were an activist for our community."

"I am an advocate for black people, same as you are. But I empathize with anyone who is treated unjustly, same as you, Ms. Story." He smiled, knowing she would have no retort.

April's phone vibrated. She read the message from Chance. "Hey, baby, can you come home early today? We need to talk."

She replied "yes" before placing the phone in her purse.

"Hey, Dr. Salek, would you mind walking me out? I want to talk to you about something."

He looked her up and down apprehensively. "What could you possibly have to talk to me about?"

April began walking toward the double doors that led out of the courtroom and motioned for him to follow her.

"So, you led a protest in front of the South Precinct yesterday..."

"I did. What about it?" he inquired.

"There was an officer, Chance Carrington, that you had words with?"

"Yeah, what about him?" he asked.

"I don't know if you know this, but he's--"

WHAM! April was knocked back and her briefcase flew from her hands, scattering papers everywhere. She looked ahead to see who had run into her. Rocky Moretti stared down at her.

"Excuse you, Rocky!" April scoffed, stepping into his face.

"No, excuse you, ambulance chaser. You send one of the good guys to jail over a criminal? Whose side are you on anyway?" he barked.

April clenched her fists at her sides. "I'm on the side of justice!"

"Really? I can't tell," he said as he brought his face so close to hers, she could feel his hot breath on her forehead.

Before she could respond, Rahim stepped between them and slammed Rocky against the door hard.

"Don't call this sister out of her name. If you want to get aggressive, do it with a man." he stated calmly.

Rocky regained his footing, but didn't approach Rahim. "Oh, so you're her protector now?" His wide eyes darted back and forth between the two of them. "How does Chance feel about your little boyfriend, April?"

Again, Rahim grabbed Rocky by the collar and slammed him into the door, this time, holding him there.

"What you're going to do now is walk out these doors and go join the rest of your department. If you say another word to this woman, you're going to need your boys to get me off you."

It was silent as Rocky weighed out his options. After several moments, he replied, "Okay. Get off me!"

Once Rahim released his grip, Rocky adjusted the disheveled collar on his uniform and stormed out the doors.

"You okay?" Rahim turned to April and looked her over.

She exhaled sharply. "Yes, I'm fine. Thank you."

She bent down to pick up her papers and he knelt next to her to help. As they gathered the documents, he waited for her to give him some insight into what had just happened, but she remained silent, clearly deep in thought.

April couldn't believe Rocky had confronted her like this. She glanced over at Rahim, thankful he had been there. When Chance got wind of this, he would take care of it. Right now, she just wanted to gather her belongings and get home.

As April and Dr. Salek exited the courtroom, the unexpected crowd erupted in cheers. News crews had assembled and the flashing of cameras was everywhere. Before she could react, a reporter stuck a microphone in her face.

"Ms. Story, congratulations on your victory in court today. Can you tell us what inspired you to take this case and how you were able to successfully prosecute it?"

"I took this case because right now in this country, there is a war on our underserved demographics. Black people and other minorities are disproportionately subjected to brutality by the people who are sworn to serve and protect them. Also, we cannot overlook the fact that poor people in general are routinely targeted for unfair and unjust treatment." She glanced at Dr. Salek who smiled and winked at her. "I wanted to show everyone that we all deserve to be treated justly and fairly. I think the jury saw that and ruled accordingly."

Again the crowd cheered and the reporter thanked her for her time. April rushed through the courthouse anxious to get home and put this entire day behind her.

April tossed her briefcase on the entry table and kicked off her heels as soon as she walked into the door. After collapsing on the couch, she stared at the ceiling, replaying the events of the day. Something told her that Rocky's behavior would not be an anomaly.

The door swung open and April could barely see Chance behind the huge bouquet of pink and red roses he was carrying. She leapt up from the couch and rushed over to help him.

"Oh my God! They are absolutely beautiful!" she exclaimed as she took the vase and walked it over to the kitchen.

The aromatic fragrance of the flowers filled her nostrils as she pruned the stems and filled the vase water. Chance walked up behind her and slipped his arms around her waist. He leaned in and kissed the back of her neck.

"I'm so proud of you, baby."

She turned her head toward him and he leaned down and kissed her lips. They stood there for a moment, lips pressed together and eyes closed, before Chance finally released his grip and headed to the bedroom to change out of his uniform. After moving the flowers into the sunny dining room, April joined him.

Neither of them said a word when April stepped into the shower. She reached for her loofah, but he gently grabbed her hand stopping her. Instead he took it and lathered it. April placed her hands on the shower wall and spread her legs as if she were being frisked. She closed her eyes savoring the moment as Chance slowly and methodically washed her from head to toe. When he reached her soft center, April tried not to shiver as he replaced the soapy loofah with his fingers and warm water. She could feel his hardness pressed against her lower back as he leaned against her and reached around to finish the job he had started. When he worked his warm, wet fingers in and out of her, careful not to miss a spot, she couldn't tell if the wetness running down her inner thighs was hers or from the shower that cascaded over them. Her breathing and heart rate sped up and she finally erupted, shaking and jerking, doing her best not to collapse onto the shower floor. Chance showed no mercy and he continued to massage and suck on the side of her neck. When her spasms finally slowed, he spun her around and stuck his tongue into her mouth forcefully. April let out an involuntary moan, turned on by his take-charge attitude. She reached out to wrap her arms around his neck, but he grabbed her wrists and pinned them against the slippery wall, kissing her harder. She tried to match his aggression but ended up leaning back and enjoying it as his mouth made love to hers. Chance released her hands and bent down to scoop her up. Now face to face with him, she pulled him in to her. This time, she kissed him long and hard, sucking and biting on his lips and tongue. He forced himself inside of her and began grinding back and forth with long, smooth strokes. April held onto his shoulders, digging in and leaving behind red scratches. He winced in pleasure and pain, but kept on stroking. They both writhed in ecstasy. As he continued to gyrate, she slid up and down the cold, damp tiles. Suddenly, an orgasm over took her and she squeezed her legs around his waist, pulsating hard around him. Right on cue, he let out a loud roar and tightened his grip on her. His erratic jerking continued until he finished releasing. He lowered her to the floor and they both washed again before exiting the bathroom.

Chance directed her to lay on the bed and pulled out a gift bag he had brought into the room and started applying Victoria's Secret Pure Seduction Body Butter all over her. The massage felt so good that April had drifted off into a light sleep. She was only awakened when Chance stopped rubbing.

"I guess that felt good," he smiled at her as she cracked open her eyes.

She smiled back and scooted up onto the pillow. "It sure did. Do you want me to do you?"

"Nah, baby. I'm good. It's your day. I'm just here to support."

"Thank you, Chance. I appreciate it."

"Oh! I almost forgot. I have something special for you!" He reached back into the gift bag and pulled out a jewelry box.

April opened the box to find a diamond tennis bracelet with a matching necklace and pair of earrings. She flipped over the bracelet to read the inscription. *WITH YOU ON MY DREAM TEAM, I COULD NEVER LOSE*

"This is beautiful. Thank you!" She leaned in and kissed him. "Come chill with me."

April returned the jewelry to the box and placed it on her nightstand. Chance slid into the bed behind her and she flipped through channels looking for a movie they could fall to sleep to. She settled on *The Notebook*, hit play and laid back into Chance's arms.

Unable to hold back, Chance grabbed the remote control, paused the movie and sat straight up.

"April, I need to talk to you about something serious."

She, too, sat up and turned to face him. "Okay. What's going on?" It had been months since he had been this affectionate toward her. *I should have known there was more to this,* she thought.

"So… you've been doing really well in your career; wouldn't you say?"

"I have. What about it, Chance?"

He was blinking his eyes excessively, a telltale sign that he was apprehensive about having this conversation.

"As you know, I'm really close to taking a big step in my career…"

"I'm aware."

"I really need a favor from you, April."

She raised her eyebrows but remained silent.

"I need you to stay away from police brutality cases until I get the job." He clasped his hands together, pleaded for her cooperation.

April's jaw dropped. "Chance! I am a prosecuting attorney! That's what I do!"

"I know. But hear me out." He moved closer and took one of her hands into his. "Baby, there are so many other people doing wrong in this world. You don't have to go after cops!"

She yanked her hand from his and stood up, unbothered by her own lack of clothing. "I do have to go after them. I have a purpose, Chance! You want me to put my career on the sideline so you can remain a part of the good old boy's club? That's what all this is about?" She gestured toward the nightstand with the gifts.

Chance stood and took her hands. "No! I got that to show you how proud I am of you and to show appreciation for how well you've dealt with my stress lately." He pulled her back over to the bed. "Here. Sit down."

She reluctantly sat on the edge of the bed and he sat next to her, never letting her hands go.

"April, we are about to spend our lives together. When I see you out here fighting for what's right and taking risks on behalf of others, I feel inadequate. I feel powerless walking the beat and just doing what I'm told!"

She softened her stance. The pain in his voice penetrated her.

"I want you to be proud of me. I want to be a partner to you. You can't be out here advocating for us while I continue to contribute to the problem."

She nodded.

"Look, I'm not asking you to give up your career, baby. Let's work together. Help me get into this position and we can work together to change things," he begged.

"I don't know what I can do to help."

"April, I'm telling you what you can do! There are a lot of people at the department who are unhappy with you going after cops. I have been under pressure to either make you stop or to leave you."

Her eyes widened. She had assumed that their relationship didn't go over well, but for him to be so blatantly accosted was shocking.

"I would never leave you for a job. I just want you to lay low for a few months and let me secure the promotion. After that I will hand over corrupt cops to you for prosecution!"

April rubbed her temples. She couldn't believe she was being asked to do this. She paced back and forth, going over the options in her mind. She loved Chance and knew he had been struggling lately.

I can't just stop taking these cases! It's only a few months, April. It won't make a difference. She stopped pacing and looked at Chance. He didn't say a word as she worked the situation out in her head. *He wants this so bad. Stop being selfish, April!*

"Ok, Chance," she forced a smile. "I will not take any more cases involving the police until you get your promotion."

He leapt up and hugged her tightly. "Thank you so much, baby. I promise you won't regret it. I'm going to make you proud."

She hugged him back, her mind racing and worrying about what the future held for them.

SACRIFICE

"Helloooooo?" Charlotte sang as she snapped her fingers in front of April's face.

April jumped to attention, dismissing the thoughts swirling around in her head. "Oh! Sorry. What were you saying, Char?"

"Have you made a decision about the Anderson case? It seems like a slam dunk for you."

April looked away. "Why don't you step up and take that one, Charlotte?"

Her mouth flew open. "I'm not ready for that! I haven't even tried a case on my own, let alone a high profile case against the police!"

Feeling the panic, April waved her hand in the air, willing Charlotte to calm down. "You're right. I will get one of the partners to take it. You can assist on it."

Charlotte stared at her blankly. "Is everything okay?"

"Of course it is. Why wouldn't it be?" April snapped.

"You live for these cases! There is no one more qualified to win than you. What's going on, April?"

"Everything is fine, Char. I just need a little break. The last trial took a lot out of me."

"That's understandable..." Charlotte conceded, but still stared her down skeptically. April was the most ambitious woman she had ever met. She never grew tired or slowed down and was always ready to fight for justice.

April slammed her laptop closed, put it into her briefcase and gathered the rest of her belongings. "As a matter of fact, I'm going to head home. I'm not feeling it today."

Before Charlotte could object, she was out the door.

April felt heavy as she exited the building. The sun beat down on her face and felt angry and burning instead of warm and comforting. As she lumbered toward the parking lot her legs weighed her down. She knew she was letting her clients down. They came to her for assistance and she was pawning them off on her colleagues. She wondered if there was a way she could help privately but resigned herself to feeling like this for the next few months.

She rummaged through her purse and pulled out her car keys. It was then that she noticed the police cruiser parked directly behind her car. Chance stood there, leaning against the car with his dark shades on and his arms folded across his chest.

"Chance! What are you doing here?" She asked as a broad smile spread across her face.

He wasn't smiling back. He slowly removed his shades and placed them in his shirt pocket. The look of disappointment was evident in his eyes.

"What's wrong? Did something happen at work? Did you hear back about the promotion already?" She held her breath, bracing herself for his bad news.

Chance put his hands up, stopping her line of questioning. "This ain't about the promotion, April."

She waited for him to continue.

"Just the other day, I spoke with you about how the so-called doctor tried to play me at the protest, right?"

She swallowed hard, knowing exactly what was coming, but nodded affirmatively.

"So imagine my surprise when Rocky shows me a news clip with you and Rahim side-by-side at a news conference..."

"Chance, we were not together--"

Again, he raised his hand to stop her. "Don't even try to lie to me. Rocky told me that you worked with ol' boy on the trial and that he was there as a member of your team."

She gasped. "That's a damn lie! I have never worked with Dr. Salek on any case. He was at the courthouse when your friend knocked my briefcase from my arm and accosted me aggressively. He stood up for me! We just happened to be walking out the courtroom at the same time when the news showed up!"

Chance grabbed his chest as if she had just stabbed him in the heart. "I met you at the house right after that. You didn't mention any of this. So you and dude are sharing secrets?"

"No!" April took a deep breath to calm herself. "I planned on telling you, Chance. After you told me that my job was a problem for you at work, I didn't want to make things worse. I was looking out for you!"

He had both hands on his head walking around in small circles. He stopped directly in front of her. He cupped her face between his hands. "I'm sorry. I should not have accused you. I'm under a lot of pressure, April. I have to guard my reputation. I cannot be humiliated in public."

She nodded again, agreeing. "I'm sorry for keeping that incident from you. I should have told you, no matter what."

"I love you, babe. I'll see you at home tonight." He kissed her on the forehead and got into his car.

She stood there watching as he sped out of the parking lot.

There was no way April could chill at the house after the unexpected confrontation with Chance. She made a detour and stopped by Janice's condo.

"To what do I owe the honor of a visit from my big sis in the middle of the day?" Janice asked as she leaned in for a hug.

"I'm off work. I just wanted to stop by and see you." April shrugged.

They sat in Janice's living room sipping wine and gossiping. It had been awhile since the sisters had an opportunity to hang out.

"Okay, so what's wrong, sis?" Janice insisted.

Knowing her sister would not give up until she had answers, April finally told her what was going on. Jan sat quietly as her sister relayed the events that had occurred after court and Chance's request that she not take particular cases. She even told her about him showing up at her job.

"So... is he checking Rocky about disrespecting you or nah?" Janice asked.

"He never brought it back up after I told him."

Janice stood up abruptly. "It's because he doesn't give a damn, sis!"

"He does care, Jan! He's just under a lot of stress right now. You don't understand what he's going through."

"Well, I'm glad you're so understanding. Does he know what you're going through? Does he know that you worked your ass off to graduate early from high school, work your way through law school and become the top prosecuting attorney in the state? Why do you have to stop your progress so he can reach his goals?" Jan fumed.

"You know it's not like that! Part of the reason I am the top prosecuting attorney is Chance. Without the inside information he has provided me over the last few years, I could never have won as many cases as I have."

"Hmph!" Jan folder her arms across her chest and looked away.

"Jan, this is how relationships work. Give and take. Chance has risked his career for mine on multiple occasions.

"You've never told me he did that, April."

"Why would I? You hate him! I couldn't risk giving you that info."

"Really, April?" You know why I don't like Chance! I thought he was a suck-up willing to turn his back on his own people to get ahead. I would have treated him totally different if I had known he was helping you from the inside."

"I know. I wish I had," April said as she stared off distantly.

Janice sat down next to her sister and held her. She hated when they argued and knew April was stressed out. *I know she's lying to make Chance look good,* she thought. *Ain't nothing she can tell me to make my me respect his ass!*

April looked over the case briefs for what seemed like the hundredth time. Charlotte had sent them over earlier in the day. It had been two months since April had announced to her colleagues that she would be taking a few months off. She couldn't bear to keep turning down cases that she knew she could win. The other attorneys in her office were surprised by the news but understood her need to take a break. Charlotte, on the other hand was not at all supportive. She suspected that something else was going on and kept asking questions but April stuck to her story about being tired.

They deleted the fucking tape! She shook her head in disbelief. *Those bastards deleted the fucking tape!* She grabbed her phone and started to dial Charlotte before realizing it was ten o'clock at night. Instead she texted her, telling her where to check for the deleted bodycam footage. According to Chance, there was always a backup tape. She was still in shock over what she had found when Chance's car finally pulled into the driveway.

April rushed to the door and was waiting with a smile by the time he climbed the stairs.

"You look happy to see me. I could get used to this," Chance beamed.

"Well don't!" April pecked him on the cheek, grabbed his hand and led him into the house.

He sat his duffle bag down and plopped down on the couch. She sat right next to him, anxious to hear about the goings on of the day.

"So… any word on whether or not you got the job?"

"Nah. It won't be announced until after the Policeman's Ball."

Her shoulders slumped and she let out an exasperated sigh.

"Don't worry, April. This will all be over soon and you can get back to work." With that he kissed her on the forehead, stood up and headed to the bedroom.

She wondered how much longer she could take sitting on the sidelines.

April traipsed up and down the aisles at Trader Joe's. This had always been one of her favorite stores, but until now, she never had time to actually enjoy the shopping experience. She had been taking her time and coming up with recipes lately. At first she had been bored, but after the first two months, she realized she may have needed a mental break. It was nice being there for Chance after a long day's work. They had become closer than they had ever been and she made a promise to herself that even when she returned to work, she would take time to stop and smell the roses.

As she stood there picking up, then putting down various packages of rice and reading the labels, a familiar voice rang out from behind her.

"Surprised to run into you here, Ms. Story."

April swung around to see Dr. Salek standing there, a red basket hanging from his arm. His fashionable glasses were gone and she could now see that his eyes were draped in the longest lashes she had ever seen on a man. He casually let them roam over her, taking in the sharp contrast in what she was wearing now versus what he was used to seeing her in. April shifted uncomfortably under his gaze and tried to inconspicuously pull her shorts down to cover more thigh. He, too, was dressed down for his trip to the grocery store. He sported a white tank top, a pair of black basketball shorts that stopped just below the knee and a matching pair of all black high-top sneakers. His sculpted arms flexed as he held on to the basket and his chiseled chest looked as if it were ready to burst out of the shirt he wore. Even clothed, she could count eight cuts in his abs. Despite his laid back appearance, his face was as smooth as silk, his hair tapered to perfection and that dimple in his right cheek, on full display. It felt wrong to even look at him.

"You look nice tonight," he attested.

April scoffed and rolled her eyes. "Yeah, right! Do I detect some sarcasm?"

He looked confused. "Not at all, Ms. Story--"

"You can call me April," she interjected. She didn't like the way her heartbeat sped up and her tummy fluttered when "Ms. Story" rolled off of his tongue.

"My apologies... April. I was not being sarcastic at all. I say what I mean and mean what I say. Just because you feel most beautiful dressed up in high end clothes with makeup on doesn't mean I am not more apt to appreciate natural beauty."

She glared at him. Who the hell was he to tell her how she felt about herself? She composed herself and pasted a smile on her face. "Thank you, Dr. Salek."

"Nah. If I'm going to call you April, you're gonna have to call me Rahim."

"Well, thanks, Rahim."

"I haven't seen you around the courthouse or on the news lately. How have you been?"

"I've been good-- actually, I've been great. I'm just taking a little time off, but I'll be back out there in the next few weeks."

He nodded affirmatively. "That's understandable. After what went down at the courthouse, I figured things had gotten pretty heavy."

April threw her head back, aghast. "That had nothing to do with it! I am not at all worried about him! Rocky does not scare me. I took a break for personal reasons."

Rahim put his hand on her shoulder. "Oh! My bad, April. I apologize for making assumptions."

His sincere look made her feel bad for overreacting. She also wanted to get his hand off of her shoulder so she could stop the warmth that was permeating her body.

"It's okay," she said as she moved out of his reach. "Speaking of the police, last time I saw you, I was going to talk to you about Officer Chance Carrington."

"You don't even have to say a thing, April. I already got the message."

Her eyes widened. "What do you mean?"

"I ran into him and he made it clear that he felt disrespected and warned me not to try and play him again."

"Oh." April was speechless. She just couldn't see Chance being confrontational like that. It was also strange that he had never mentioned the incident to her.

"He also let me know that you were his fiancé and told me to stay away from you."

This time her mouth flew open. She could feel the color drain from her face and wanted to sink into the tile floor and disappear.

"Where did you run into him at?"

Rahim looked amused. He realized that Chance had never shared the incident with his "beloved fiancé".

"Our Lives Count has been meeting with a police department to try and come up with a way to prevent the killing of unarmed black men."

April took a step back. Now she was in the twilight zone. "Okay, what does this have to do with Chance?"

Rahim looked around ready to exit the conversation. There must have been a reason the man had neglected to share this information with his woman. He didn't want to find himself in the middle of any drama. He was about to make an excuse and leave, but when he looked back at April, something in her expression made him feel like she really needed to know. For some reason, he just couldn't find it in his heart to tell her no.

He sighed long and hard before continuing. "As you probably know, the city just hired its first black female Chief of Police, Candice Reynolds."

She nodded.

"She's new but she's aggressively going after this problem, so she requested a meeting with me. She wanted to meet in the restaurant at the Sheraton Hotel downtown."

Now April hung on his every word.

"When I arrived to meet her, she was already there, seated with… Officer Carrington. She told me that he was her trusted advisor and that they would be working closely together on this project."

April couldn't believe what she was hearing. When the Chief of Police was selected a month and a half ago, she was excited and hoped it meant a change was coming. She had asked Chance repeatedly if he had met her. When he said no, she practically begged him to make contact so he could introduce her.

"How long ago was this meeting?" April demanded, now obviously upset.

Rahim wished like hell he had just walked away. "Well, the first meeting--"

"The first meeting? You mean there was more than one?" She was about to blow a fuse.

He paused and tried to figure out whether her anger was directed at him or at the situation.

"The first meeting was about six weeks ago. Right after she took office. We've been meeting twice a week in the evening ever since."

April stumbled backwards and grabbed her chest. It felt as if she had been hit with a ton of bricks. Chance had been getting in late a couple of times a week, but he'd told her he was working overtime to look good for the promotion. He had never mentioned any of this. She had so many questions, but reminded herself that Rahim was not one of her home girls. There was no way she was going to make herself look any worse than she already did in front of a virtual stranger.

"Well, thanks for that. It was good seeing you." She turned on her heels, leaving her basket full of groceries parked in the middle of the aisle.

April held back tears as she ran to her car. She was fumbling for the key when Rahim jogged up.

"Hey!"

She turned around wondering what more he wanted.

"I'm sorry if I said anything in there that upset you. It wasn't my intention."

"Wasn't it though? I saw the look on your face when you told me. You were damn near giddy!"

He cracked a slight smile. "Okay. I'll admit that your boyfriend following me into the bathroom and playing tough guy with me irritated me. I enjoyed causing a problem for him."

"Exactly!" April said as she finally located her key and opened the door.

"Wait!" He grabbed her arm. "I hated seeing you upset. For that, I'm sorry."

"Thanks." She got in, started the car and threw it in reverse.

Still standing there, he tapped on her window and she rolled it down.

"What?"

"Look, I don't know what your man thinks my intentions were toward you, but I really just admired you professionally and wanted to work with you." He reached out to hand her his card and she stared at his outstretched hand.

"Please, April. I promise, I am not trying to cause any trouble. We can help each other. If you have the ability to work with me in any capacity, let me know. If not, I completely understand."

She finally took the card and stuck in her purse before rolling up the window and peeling out of the parking lot. The tears that she had held at bay freely spilled down her cheeks as she sped toward what was supposed to be home.

April dialed Chance frantically over and over. Every time he didn't pick up the phone, she became more incensed. Finally, her phone dinged and a text from him popped up on the screen.

WORKING LATE TONIGHT, BABY. I'LL CALL YOU LATER.

She tossed the phone on the passenger seat and screamed as she gripped the steering wheel tight. She slowed down, not wanting to go to an empty house.

"Hello," Charlotte groggily muttered as she picked up the phone.

"I'm sorry, Char. I didn't know you were sleeping."

"April! I've been worried about you! I haven't heard from you in days."

"I know. I'm sorry. Can I come over and talk?"

"Of course! I'll be waiting."

Usually April would talk to Jan when she had a problem, but she wasn't in the mood to hear "I told you so". She and Charlotte had grown close over the few years they had worked together. She hadn't ever shared details about her relationship, but really needed to talk to someone.

Charlotte answered the door looking exactly as April would have expected her to. She sported flannel pink pajamas with *Hello Kitty* all over them. Her frizzy red curls were pulled back into a messy ponytail and without a drop of makeup, her bright red freckles really stood out against her pale skin. April brushed by.

"Well, come on in!" Charlotte joked.

"Sorry. I didn't mean to be rude. I am just so pissed right now, Char!"

She relayed the details of the past few months; Chance asking her to hold back on the police brutality cases, his opportunity to be Assistant Chief of Police, and his plan to help change things once he made it.

"Wow!" Charlotte sat astonished. "That's really heavy, April. I am surprised that you agreed to that. You love your work!"

"I do, Char. I just wanted to give my man a win. I figured a few months off would do me some good."

"I get that. So what seems to be the problem?"

"Everything was fine until today. Remember I told you about the Our Lives Count meeting that I attended with Janice?"

Charlotte nodded.

April went on to tell her about Rahim, the incident with Rocky at the courthouse and what she had just heard about Chance and the new Chief of Police.

After she finished, they both sat quietly digesting the story.

"So, what are you going to do now?" Charlotte finally asked.

"When I see him, I am going off, Char! How dare he have me put my career on the backburner so he can gallivant around with her!"

"I understand. That's exactly what I would do. His dishonesty is unacceptable. It was a big thing for you to put him before your career."

It's settled then. I'm not crazy! I can't wait to see his lying ass!

Chance was still sleeping peacefully. He usually slept in on Saturdays. April noted that his face looked as if he didn't have a care in the world. She, on the other hand had stayed up all night. She tossed and turned wondering what exactly was going on with Chance. Why had he lied to her? What was his relationship with Candice Reynolds? Once again, she glanced at him and thought about tossing her glass of water on the bedside table right into his face. Instead she rolled over and put the pillow over her face to block out the sunlight streaming through the blinds.

"Good morning!" Chance exclaimed exuberantly.

I just fell to sleep! Nevertheless, April removed the pillow from her face and stared up at him.

He had the same smile he had been wearing for the last few weeks. It pissed her off to know that she wasn't the reason for his newfound happiness. She sat up as he placed a tray across her lap. There were pancakes, sunny-side-up eggs and turkey bacon. He had poured a glass of orange juice garnished with a strawberry on the rim.

"Thank you," she forced herself to say.

"You're very welcome," he said. He sat down on the edge of the bed. "I've been wanting to talk to you about something, April."

For the first time since last night, she made eye contact with him.

"Oh? Is something wrong?"

He cleared his throat. "No-- not necessarily. It's just that I have something in the works that I haven't shared--"

He was interrupted by his phone ringing. He picked it up immediately, stood up and rushed out of the bedroom to take the call. April sat with her arms folded listening to his muffled voice and straining to hear what he was talking about to no avail.

After a few minutes, the door swung open and he rushed in and grabbed his car keys.

"We'll have to pick this up later, baby." He leaned in, planted a kiss on her temple and was back out the door before she could object.

April sat the tray aside and jumped out of bed, rushing to the living room window just in time to see him backing out the driveway while having an intense conversation on the phone.

Forget this! I'm done with this!

April yanked the hair tie off her hair and rushed into the bathroom. She turned the water on and the temperature up until it just about scalded her. She needed to feel the heat of the hot water on her body to melt away the shame she was feeling at her own stupidity. She washed her hair and scrubbed the stench of housewife from her body. After blow-drying her hair, slicking it back into a sleek ponytail and moisturizing her skin, she stepped into her walk-in closet, grabbed a navy blue pencil skirt and a matching button up chiffon blouse. She wanted to be comfortable, so instead of her usual stilettos, she put on a pair of Michael Kors t-strap platform sandals. Standing in front of the full-length mirror, she marveled at her transformation back into herself.

Now that's what I'm talking about! She mumbled.

With that, April grabbed her keys and ran out the front door.

She walked through the lobby and the receptionist greeted her gleefully. "Good morning, Ms. Story! Good to see you back!"

Everyone else looked as if they had seen a ghost. They stopped what they were doing and stared wide-mouthed at her. Charlotte was across the office giving the file clerk detailed instructions as usual. She did a double take when April crossed the office and rushed after her.

When she turned the key and walked into her office, it was a relief to find all of her things exactly as she had left them. The room could use a good dusting, but felt like home.

"April, what the heck are you doing here?" Charlotte asked.

"Geez, don't be so happy to see me, Char!"

"I am happy to see you. It's just... after last night's conversation, I don't know what this means. Did you confront Chance?"

"Nope!"

"April!"

"I thought it over and decided not to bother." April shrugged.

Charlotte looked confused. "Wait a minute... As upset as you were last night, you're suddenly not worried?"

"Not necessarily. I just want to watch and see what happens. I think he was going to tell me this morning, but he had to go. He's running around with the Chief of Police. He is trying to run for Assistant Chief of Police. It could be completely innocent."

"Okay. If you think it may be innocent, what are you doing back here? Has Chance gotten the position?"

"Not yet. But if the position depends on me dropping everything I've worked hard for, it may not be meant to be."

Charlotte chuckled at April trying to sound so tough. "So, you're ready to take on a case right now."

It was like the wind left April's sails. "Not yet. I'm going to be in the office helping behind the scenes but will wait until after he gets the job to take cases."

"Uh huh... not so nonchalant after all?" Charlotte joked much to April's chagrin. "Follow me. I'll update you on the current cases."

Charlotte filled her in and she asked questions as they made the trek across the office. Charlotte's phone was ringing as soon as they stepped into her office. She hit the speaker button and the receptionist announced that their client had arrived.

"Just in time! Send him in." Charlotte rubbed her hands, clearly excited about the guest.

"Who is it?" April demanded.

Charlotte didn't say a word, but walked over to open the door.

"Thanks for coming. It's good to see you," she greeted as she stretched out her hand.

April was shocked when Tariq walked into the office. "Tariq? What are you doing here?"

A look of confusion spread over his face. He looked back and forth between she and Charlotte.

"April, Tariq has retained us in a lawsuit against the city. We think we can prove that Officer Moretti framed and arrested him unlawfully. If we can convict him of that, the lawsuit will be effortless."

Alarm spread over her face. "But Chance was there, too. If you throw Rocky under the bus, you will have to throw him under!"

Tariq diverted his eyes and Charlotte walked forward taking April by the shoulders. "I am fully aware of what this means for Chance. Tariq is not going after him, but he may be collateral damage."

April looked at Tariq, silently pleading with him not to proceed.

"Sis, you know I love you. I love you and Chance. But what happened to me was wrong. What he allowed to happen to me was wrong. I lost everything. There's a price to pay." His eyes pierced her and she knew there was no changing his mind.

Tears welled in her eyes and she massaged her throbbing temples. She hated the fact that two people she cared about were on the outs.

Tariq moved closer and took her hands into his. "Look, April. This is why I came to y'all. If there is a way to get Rocky without getting Chance, I'm all for it, but somebody has to pay for what happened. Did I do the right thing by coming here? Can I trust you?"

April gasped. "Oh my God, Tariq! You know you can trust me! I would never mess up a case for personal reasons. I understand where you're coming from and want to help you… and Chance."

Tariq smiled and hugged her. "Thanks, sis."

After he finally left, April glared at Charlotte. "Why didn't you tell me that you had taken on Tariq as a client?"

Charlotte rolled her eyes. "Honestly, it just happened. Also, after you said you needed a break from work, I didn't want to stress you out."

"I understand."

"There is something else I need to tell you."

"What now, Charlotte?"

"An investigation has been opened… well several investigations… but we think we have enough evidence to prosecute Rocky in the shooting involving the domestic incident a while back."

April choked on her coffee. "What?"

"There has been an investigation going on for months and the shooting doesn't seem to be justified."

"That can't be! That investigation was closed."

"It was never closed. Some evidence didn't match with the statements given by Rocky."

"What about Chance?"

"I don't know about him. He is not being prosecuted now, but I can't speak for the future."

April's heart raced. This was too much news to take in all at once. Chance had no idea what kind of trouble he could be in. She knew that everything Rocky had done would come back to haunt him. She wished Chance had cut him off a long time ago.

"You said several cases..."

"Yes. Every shooting he has been involved in is being looked at right now."

April felt sick to her stomach. She needed time to think. Her entire world as she knew it had just imploded.

"I need to go home."

"Do you need me to drive you," Charlotte asked.

"No. I'll be fine." April headed for the door.

Charlotte grabbed her arm stopping her. "April, I know Chance is your fiancé, but I need you to understand that everything we have discussed is confidential."

"I know." With that she stalked out of the office.

SECRETS

It had been two days since April had secretly returned to work. Things had been no different between her and Chance. She would get home before him and he had worked late every night. Charlotte would send her notes on the case and she would do research and present ideas. There had to be a way to get a win for Tariq while keeping Chance out of the crossfire.

"No dinner?" Chance asked irritably as he came in.

April slammed her laptop closed and jammed her papers into her briefcase. "Hey, Chance. I'm sorry. I lost track of time." She rushed into the kitchen to try and throw a quick meal together.

"Lately, you've been losing track of time a lot. You ain't made a decent meal in days."

It took everything in her not to go off. "My bad, Chance. I'm not a professional housewife. I'm doing the best I can," she snapped.

"Are you, April? I'm working hard to get to the next level, but over the last few days, it doesn't look like you've done anything around the house. You're in sweatpants every time I walk in the door. Can't you at least try and make me want to come home to you?"

Her head snapped in his direction. She was livid. "Who the hell do you think you're talking to, Chance? I'm not some low-budget broad that needs you to take care of me! I'm doing you a favor! Don't you ever fix your mouth to disrespect me again." She was inches from him pointing a finger in his face.

They stared each other down for several moments. Finally, Chance blinked first and rushed into the bedroom, slamming the door behind him.

Who does he think he is? Now I know something is going on between him and the Police Chief. He has never treated me like this!

She didn't even bother grabbing a pillow and blanket before tossing herself on the overstuffed couch. She tossed and turned in the pitch dark for hours trying to make sense of what had transpired between her and Chance. Other than a few hushed conversations behind the closed door, he hadn't even bothered to peep out and see if she was coming to bed.

"April?"

She had finally fallen asleep at four in the morning and the last thing she needed was someone waking her up.

"April?" Chance repeated as he gently nudged her.

"Yeah, Chance," she grumbled.

"You awake?"

"I am now!" She flipped over to face him. "What's up?"

"I wanted to apologize about how I talked to you last night. I appreciate the sacrifice you're making for me... for us. I want you to know I didn't mean any it."

April didn't say a word. She looked in his eyes to determine whether or not he was being genuine, but all she saw was a liar looking back at her. She had the urge to call him out, but decided she was too tired to argue.

"Cool, Chance. Have a good day." She rolled back over without giving him time to respond.

He sat there watching the back of her head for a while. Knowing he was hoping she would turn back over and tell him that all was forgiven, April pretended to snore lightly. Finally, she heard the door close behind him.

She picked up the phone and dialed. "Hey, Char. I'm gonna stay home today. I'm not feeling well."

"Oh, no! Do you need me to bring you anything?" Charlotte offered.

"No. But thank you. It's nothing a little rest won't cure."

After hanging up, she drifted into a deep slumber.

BANG! BANG! BANG!

April startled awake. She picked up her phone and looked at the time. It was 6:35pm.

"Oh, shit!" she shrieked as she sat up on the couch. "Who is it?" she yelled.

No response.

She tiptoed to the front door and looked out the peephole. Begrudgingly, she turned the deadbolt and opened the door.

"Tariq! What are you doing here?"

He looked into the house behind her and then shot glances over his shoulders. "I'm sorry for popping up, April. I didn't know what else to do."

She scrunched her face up, confused. "Come inside." She grabbed him by his wrist and pulled him in.

Once in the foyer, he paced back and forth.

"Tariq, what is going on?" she demanded.

He stopped moving and looked at her stone-faced. "Have you told Chance anything about the case I'm bringing against Rocky or the investigation?"

"Of course not! Why would you even ask that?"

"Last night, someone shot my house up. I had to send my girl to stay at her mom's," he explained.

April gripped her chest. "That's crazy! Did you call the police?"

He shot her a condescending look. "Really? You really think I called the cops?"

She folded her arms across her chest defiantly. "So what did you do, Tariq?"

"I got my important shit and got out of there."

"Good. I'm glad no one got hurt."

"But that's not it. Tonight, someone in an unmarked car tried to run me off the road."

April didn't even bother inquiring about who he thought it was. Both she and Tariq had come to the same conclusion.

"But why would Rocky come after you? How would he even know?"

"People talk, April. Ain't no telling, but I gotta lay low until he's locked up."

She was the one doing the pacing now. "Go to my parents' house."

Tariq frowned. "I can't impose on your mom and dad like that, April."

April wouldn't take no for an answer. "They love you like a son, Tariq. I'm going to call and let them know you're on your way. Don't tell anybody you're there."

"Of course not." He stuck his head out the front door and surveyed the neighborhood before swiftly pacing back around the corner to his car.

April leaned against the door. Everything was happening so fast. She needed to get in control before it was too late.

No sooner than she had sat back on the couch, Chance whipped into the driveway. April sighed, not looking forward to picking up where they had left off this morning.

Chance burst into the door with an arm full of roses and some Mexican food.

"Hey, baby. How was your day?" he cheerfully asked.

"Fine." April murmured. "Yours?"

"It was good. You hungry?"

She didn't reply, but watched him as he zipped around the kitchen, putting the roses in a vase and piling food onto plates.

Finally, he sat a plate and a glass of Chardonnay down in front of her before joining her on the couch.

"I want to talk to you about something."

"Okay, I'm listening," April replied as she pushed the food around on her plate with the fork. She pretended to be nonchalant but was eager to hear what he had to say.

"Remember you asked me about introducing you to Candice Reynolds?" he asked.

"Who is that?" April decided to play dumb.

"Only the first woman Chief of Police in the city!" He exclaimed.

"Oh, that's right. What about her?"

He smiled broadly. "Well, I finally got an opportunity to speak with her today. If-- when I get this position, I'll be working right under her, so I'll have her ear."

April grinned. "That's great, Chance. I'm surprised you are just now meeting her. She's got hired a couple of months ago."

His eyes darted around. "Yeah, it takes a while to get settled, so she is just now making time for introductions."

You are such a liar! April thought as she looked at him. The only reason she could come up with for his dishonesty was that he was having an affair with the woman.

"Well, I'm glad to hear it." She clicked on the television and sat back watching the news.

April had left for work as soon as Chance left the house this morning. Today was important and she wanted to get in and out as early as possible. She had even made the drive to her parents' house to check on Tariq. Satisfied that all was well, she rushed home to get ready.

Although the shower was running, April could hear Chance come in and move about the house. The shower in the guest bathroom on the other side of the wall turned on so she knew he was getting prepared for the evening, too. She had decided to get dressed in the bathroom so she could step out and wow him with her look.

April gave herself a once over before exiting the bathroom. Her floor-length formal gown was royal blue and sparkled. It was strapless and showed just enough cleavage to be sexy but appropriate. She had beat her face to perfection put her hair up into a high ponytail with curly tendrils falling down to frame her delicate face. She slipped into a pair of matching open-toe stilettos.

Looking around the bedroom, she didn't see any sign of Chance. April entered the living room to find him standing in front of the mirror doing one final adjustment to his tie. When he noticed her behind him, he spun around to take in her look.

"Wow! You look stunning!" he beamed.

"You don't look so bad yourself," she mused.

Chance had on a black tuxedo, perfectly tailored to fit his body. Coincidentally, he had on a blue shirt that went well with her dress. He had a fresh fade that blended into his tapered and lined facial hair. He could be on the cover of GQ magazine.

"Where are you going?" he asked.

April laughed. "Very funny. Let's get out of here."

"No, April. I'm serious. Where are you going?"

"To the Policeman's Ball with you! The same place we go every year around this time."

He ran his hand over his face in frustration. "I'm sorry. I thought we discussed this."

"Discussed what?"

He took both of her hands in his. "The entire department will be at this event. I told you that some decision-makers had an issue with what your office was doing. It just isn't a good time to show up with you on my arm."

She snatched her hands from his and backed up. "So you're ashamed of me?"

"Not at all, April! I'm just being strategic. We have a plan. We just gotta make a few sacrifices to make it happen."

"*We* have to make sacrifices, Chance?" she shot back. "That's interesting because the only person I see making any sacrifices is me."

"Is that right? How can you say that? I've risked my job too many times to count to get you information you needed to win your cases. That's not sacrifice?"

"It is. But what about defending me and protecting me? I would never let anyone tell me what I can or cannot do with you. No one can disrespect you in my presence."

Chance rolled his eyes. "You're being dramatic. Clearly this is a different situation."

"Clearly." April sat on the couch.

Chance started to say something else but decided against it. Instead, he waved her off, turned and left.

April sat on the couch feeling like a fool. She was dressed to the nines for an event she was never invited to. The annual Policeman's Ball was for the who's who of Seattle. Everyone dressed to impress and everybody who was anybody would be in attendance. It was even broadcast on the local access channel. This would be the first time in five years she was not welcome. She didn't bother changing. She walked over to the kitchen and poured a glass of Grey Goose. Usually she mixed her drinks, but tonight, April needed it straight up.

Her mind was racing and she couldn't find anything on TV to distract her from herself. She was on her third drink and definitely feeling it. The more she thought about the way that Chance had dismissed her, the angrier she got. Out of curiosity, she finally flipped to Channel Nine's coverage of the ball. After watching various movers and shakers arrive, she squinted unable to believe her eyes. A black limo pulled up and Chance exited. He took a moment to flash a brilliant smile at the cameras before walking around to the other side of the car. He opened the door and reached in to help her out. Candice Reynolds. She, too, wore a royal blue ball gown that matched his outfit, although hers was long-sleeved. She was a nice-looking woman, but couldn't hold a candle to April. Cameramen crowded around, getting as many photos as they could of the glamorous couple.

"Ms. Reynolds, congratulations on your new job," a reporter said as he aimed his microphone to her for a response.

"Thank you. I'm just happy to have an opportunity to serve the people of the City of Seattle."

"And we are glad to have you on board. Who is this handsome man accompanying you this evening?"

"This is Officer Chance Carrington of the South Precinct. He has several years on the force and is currently in the running for Assistant Chief of Police."

The cameras and reporters all turned their attention to him.

"Mr. Carrington, why do you believe you are the best candidate for Assistant Chief of Police?"

"I've dreamed my entire life of giving back to my community. My father was…"

"Blah, blah, fucking blah!" April shouted as she turned off the TV and threw the remote control at it.

Bastard! She stumbled over to the dining room table to retrieve her purse. Fumbling around inside, she finally found her keys. *He thinks he can do me like this? I'll show him! I'm going to the ball!*

She wobbled to the front door. Before she turned the knob she came to her senses. *Oh my God! I'm drunk. What the hell am I doing? I can't embarrass myself like this.* She opened her purse to put the keys back in and caught a glimpse of the card with Dr. Salek's name printed across it.

April plopped back down on the couch and dialed the number. Halfway through the first ring she glanced and the clock and frantically hit the end button. She'd had no idea it was almost eleven at night.

Immediately the phone began to ring. It was him. *Shoot!* It rang three times before she finally got the nerve to pick it up.

"Hello?"

"Ms. Story. You finally called me." He sounded awfully cheerful for this time of night.

"April-- call me April. And how did you know it was me?"

"Name ID, of course," he laughed.

She slammed herself against the back of the couch. "I'm so sorry for calling so late, Rahim. I lost track of time."

"No need to apologize, Ms.-- April. I was wide awake. I do my best work after hours." Something in the tone of his voice made the last comment sound inappropriate.

"Anyway, how are you doing?" he continued.

"I'm good."

"You sure?" He sounded skeptical. "I would have thought you would be at the big Policeman's Ball with your fiancé tonight."

"Yeah, well... you thought wrong," she quipped.

"Whoa! My bad. I didn't mean to intrude."

She exhaled loudly into the phone. "No, please don't apologize. It's my fault. Can I be honest with you?"

"Please do..." he prodded.

"I'm having a really shitty night. I wanted to talk to someone-- someone who was unbiased, so I called you. I don't know why, but I did."

The line went silent and she immediately wished she hadn't overshared.

"I'm glad you did," he finally answered.

Again, there was dead silence on the phone.

"Hey, you want to meet me by the water for a quick bite so we can talk?" he asked.

I do... but I shouldn't. If Chance finds out, I'll never hear the end of it. She thought. *You know what? Fuck Chance!*

"Sure. I'll be there in fifteen minutes."

"Bet," he said before hanging up.

April went into the bathroom and splashed water on her face to sober up before darting out the front door.

She could see him leaning on the railing and staring out at the water when she pulled up. Even in the dark of night his features stood out. He walked over and opened her door after she had parked.

"Dang! All dressed up just to come chat with me?"

April looked down at her ball gown and started laughing hysterically. She was so tipsy; she had forgotten she had it on. Now she was out here on the dock in the middle of the night looking crazy as hell. Rahim couldn't help but smile at her contagious laugh. He took off his jacket and wrapped it around her shoulders. She could still feel the warmth from his body in the garment and the fresh scent he wore enveloped her.

They just stood on the dock for a while taking in the peaceful surroundings. Her mind raced and her anxiety took over. April couldn't believe everything happening right now. Chance had always been honest and loyal. He had always put her before his job. Things were changing so quickly and she was scared to death about where this would end.

"You want go inside and grab a bite?" Rahim asked, snapping her back into the moment.

They went into the twenty-four-hour burger joint, ordered food and slid into a booth. Rahim watched her as she scarfed down the greasy burger and fries.

"That should balance out the liquor in your system and make you feel better."

April stopped chewing and stared him down. "What makes you think I'm drunk or not feeling well."

He chuckled. "I never said you were drunk. But it's clear you had a few drinks tonight."

She bowed her head. *What am I doing? I should never have let this man… this stranger see me like this.* She had lost her appetite.

"And I don't know you that well, but I pick up on energy and aura. It's obvious that you're not yourself."

"You're right. I'm in my feelings and I shouldn't have called you in the middle of the night or had you come out to meet me."

He frowned. "What? No. That's not at all what I am saying. I'm glad you called me. I would have preferred to have picked you up because I don't want you driving after drinking, but it's good, April."

She laughed. "Thank you for coming then… and for finally dropping the *Ms. Story* thing."

"I catch on eventually… and what wrong with addressing you respectfully?"

"Nothing. I just feel like that's probably how you talk to women in general. I don't want to be just another lady you're impressing with your chivalrous ways."

He burst out cracking up. "My chivalrous ways? You are something else. I didn't know you cared how I treat other women, April."

She stopped smiling. "I-- I didn't mean it like that, she stuttered. "I was just playing around."

His eyes danced around. He seemed amused by her discomfort and unwilling to let her off the hook as she attempted to explain where she was coming from.

April cleared her throat. "So what business of yours did you want to talk about?"

"Oh yeah! So I have an idea and want to get some input on it."

"Okay?"

He sat up straight. "As I told you when I saw you last, I've been meeting with the Chief of Police in an effort to solve the police brutality problem..."

April bristled. The mention of the woman pissed her off. She had wanted to connect with her and see if they could work together, but now that she was sneaking around with Chance, it would never happen.

"What does your meeting with her have to do with me?" April asked.

"Well, she is looking for some ideas on how to lower the chances of these things happening. I want to offer suggestions, but mine are usually militant or just wishful thinking. I need to come up with some sensible, well-thought out solutions that she can get behind."

"That's great, Rahim. I'm glad you realize where you fall short. That's an important step in making progress."

"Thank you. I want to get your input. You've been working in and against the system for years. You know your way around the law. I need you to help me provide realistic suggestions that make sense."

She placed her hand over her heart. "I'm flattered that you would come to me with this. What makes you think I would want to help?"

He smirked at her. "Come on, April. You go hard for your clients... a lot of them pro bono. Watching you in the courtroom, anybody can see that you're not afraid to fight and you know your stuff. You're not inspired by money. You just want to do what's right. But if you need me to pay you for your time, I'm willing to do that."

"No! I don't need to be paid for helping."

"Cool. You should also know I'm not trying to steal your ideas. I will make sure both of us get credit for whatever we accomplish."

She waved him off. "I don't care about that. I would be honored to assist with getting this done."

Without hesitation, he pulled out a pen and notepad. They talked about the possibility of fining police officers that turned off their body cams while on duty or setting up an unbiased unit to look into matters of police violence against citizens. They had been engrossed in the discussion for over an hour when April's phone started to ring. She rolled her eyes but accepted the call.

"Hey, where are you?" Chance asked before she could say anything.

"I'm out and about. What's up?"

He paused. "So you're upset with me?"

"Not at all. What's up, Chance?"

"I just got home and saw that you weren't here. Since it's after midnight, I got worried."

She pulled the phone from her face and looked at the time.

"Well, I'm fine. Thanks for checking. See you later."

"Wait!" he blurted out before she could disconnect the call. "I'm gonna wait up for you to make sure you get in safely."

"Do whatever you want, Chance." She hung up.

Rahim kept his eyes on the notepad jotting down notes and pretending not to have listened to her phone call.

"Let's talk more about what the fines would look like," he said.

"Actually, I'm going to have to pick this up another time. It's late and I need to get home."

"Understood," he said as he slipped out of the booth and stood up. He reached out to take her hand and helped her to her feet.

"Thank you," she said. *He is such a gentleman. And he's fine as hell. Any woman that finally locks him down will be lucky.*

He walked her to her car and once again opened the door.

She was backing out when he waved for her to stop. She rolled down the window wondering what was wrong.

"I just wanted to say that I really admire your strength and your ambition. You're a beautiful person both inside and out. I ain't gotta know you to see all of that. Don't let anybody change who you are, April. You're perfect."

He turned around and walked away and she was glad he did. She didn't know how to react to what he had said. The words replayed in her head over and over again on her way home.

When April arrived at her house she could see dim light shining from the living room and Chance's silhouette moving around. She parked and started toward the front door before realizing she was still wearing Rahim's jacket. She did a one eighty and returned to her car to leave it in the trunk.

"Where you been, April?" Chance demanded as soon as she stepped in the door.

"Why?" she asked.

"Why? Because it's not normal for you to be out until one o'clock in the morning without telling me where you are. When did this start?"

She scoffed. "I guess it started the same night you decided that you would rather take the Chief of Police to the most important event of the year instead of me."

"April, I can explain…"

"Don't bother, Chance," she snapped before turning and heading into the bedroom.

She slammed the door behind her, undressed and washed her face before sprawling out across the bed alone. She stared up at the ceiling wondering why Rahim had said those things to her. For some reason the fact that he thought she was perfect felt good. *He probably tells that to every woman he meets,* she decided. Nevertheless, she had a smile on her face as she drifted off to sleep.

Chance had pleaded his case multiple times over the last few days. Every time he explained himself and apologized, April told him there was no need. He thought she was only saying that because she was hurt or upset, but really, it was fine.

She understood how he could want to be around someone who understood him. Candice Reynolds was in his line of work; they would likely be working closely together for many years to come. It was only a matter of time before Chance came home and announced that he was leaving April for her or someone like her.

They had been a mismatch from the beginning. According to her mother and father, April, like her sister, was born an activist. She was always trying to offset her privileged upper class upbringing by fighting for people less fortunate; people who looked like her. Once she started, she couldn't stop. She believed she had been blessed with a good life and that it was her job to give back.

Chance, on the other hand, had spent his life trying to escape the hood. Although his father and his half-siblings lived a good life, he and his mother had been left behind to fend for themselves. He had always tried to do something, anything, that would finally make his dad believe that he was good enough, but falling short.

When he and April met and fell for one another, he finally cared about something other than living up to his absent father's expectations. Although they were different, the love they shared made them respect one another and understand each other. She had thought that love was enough to sustain the relationship. Now it seemed like Chance would do anything to get to where he wanted to be. Nothing would stand in his way... including her.

STAND FOR SOMETHING

"We picked him up this morning. He and his fiancée will be staying here until everything blows over."

"Thank you so much, Rahim! I owe you one."

"No problem at all! I'm glad we could help the brother out. That's what we're here for. Here he comes now. I'm gonna let you holla at him."

"Aye, sis."

"Tariq, I'm glad y'all are safe."

"No doubt. I couldn't stand the thought of putting Mr. and Mrs. Story in danger. This spot is nice."

"Alright. Y'all get some rest."

Working late tonight. Can't wait to see you. April read the message that Chance had sent.

"Yeah, right," April mumbled.

It was Friday night and once again, she had been left home alone. She popped some popcorn, poured herself a glass of ginger ale and curled up on the couch to watch *Girls' Trip*.

She almost choked laugh at Tiffany Haddish being obnoxious in the airport. The phone rang and she paused the movie.

"Ha! Hello?"

"Sounds like I interrupted you in the middle of a good time. You want me to call you back?"

She giggled. "No, you're fine. I'm just watching *Girls' Trip* for the third time."

"Yeah, that movie was funny as hell."

"To what do I owe this phone call, Rahim?"

"I was just up and wanted to talk."

"Interesting. How did you know my man wasn't sitting right next to me?"

"Trust me, I know."

April guessed he knew something she didn't know about Chance's whereabouts, but decided not to ruin her night by asking.

"Okay then. Let's talk."

She got comfortable on the couch and kicked her feet up on the arm of the couch as they chatted. His voice had dropped an octave and April could imagine him lying down in a wife-beater looking sexy as hell. She brushed the thought from her mind and tried to be as innocent as an engaged woman on the phone with a handsome single man late on a Friday night could be. Before she knew it, hours had passed and she had to let him go. Neither April nor Rahim had spent all night on the phone since high school. They said their good nights and hung up.

Chance quietly crept into the house around one in the morning. He tiptoed past April on the couch, trying not to wake her. She listened to him shuffling around but pretended to be asleep.

April was surprised to find Chance in the kitchen working on his laptop and sipping coffee when she got home in the early afternoon. Usually on Wednesdays he claimed to be picking up extra shifts doing security.

"Hey! What are you doing home so early?"

He looked up from his work. "Don't be so happy to see me."

"I'm just not used to seeing you during the day anymore."

He stood up and walked over to her, wrapping his arms around her tightly.

"I know baby. I'm sorry that I've been all wrapped up in this work situation and haven't given us the attention we need. I'm sorry."

He leaned in and kissed her lips lightly. It had been weeks since they had shown one another any affection and she was not sure how to react. Chance held her in his arms and rested his face against hers. April awkwardly held onto him. He placed his hands on her shoulders and put some space between them.

"I want to take you out to make up for it," he offered.

"What do you have in mind?" she asked.

"I know you've been wanting to go to Palisades for dinner. Go get dressed and I'm going to take you out."

Unable to say no when Chance was being so assertive, she went to the room, put on a short, red, flirty dress and was ready to go in a zip.

They talked non-stop on the way to the restaurant. Chance seemed to be back to his old self. He opened up about trying to make a good impression on the Police Chief, but stopped short of admitting that he had been spending an extensive amount of time with her. April kept reminding herself that he was still lying to her every time she found herself laughing at his jokes.

The valet took the car and Chance escorted her into the restaurant. They sat in a booth where the lights were low. The ambience immediately put April at ease. She watched while he ordered their dinner and thought about how much she had missed spending time with him.

When their meals arrived the delectable aromas of crab in garlic and butter sauce wafted into April's nose. She dug in while sipping on a margarita. She and Chance were deep in conversation when a familiar figure approached. The hair on the back of her neck stood up.

"What's up, Chance?"

Chance looked around to see who had called his name.

"Hey! What up, Roc?"

Chance stood up and he and Rocky embraced one another. As soon as Chance returned to his seat, Rocky turned his attention to April.

"I'm surprised to see you here with her. I thought you had kicked her to the curb."

April frowned and looked at Chance. He shot his eyes everywhere around the room but refused to look her in the eye.

"Roc, don't start this, bro. This ain't the time or the place."

April fumed. "Well, when is the time or the place, Chance? I'm surprised to see you still even speaking to him after I told you how he treated me at the courthouse!"

"This is my guy. He'll never cut me off. You, on the other hand are just a bi-- a female. He can get another," Rocky laughed.

Chance leapt from his seat and grabbed a handful of Rocky's shirt. "You being real disrespectful right now and you need to go on about your business."

Rocky threw his hands in the air. "My bad, bro. I'm just trying to look out for you. Besides, she already has a man to defend her honor. Ain't that right, April?"

She grabbed her margarita off the table and splashed the entire drink in his face. He lunged at her, but Chance held on and pushed him in the other direction.

"Her and her friends are trying to make me lose my career and get me locked up! Her firm keeps coming after people on the force. One day it's gonna be you, Chance! You're gonna have to make a decision, bro. You can't play both sides of the fence."

He yanked his shirt away from Chance and stormed out of the restaurant. Everyone had stopped eating and had their eyes glued on April and Chance. She had never been so humiliated in her life.

Chance walked over and slipped an arm around her waist. "I'm sorry that happened, baby." He kissed her cheek. "Let's enjoy the rest of our meal."

April moved out of his grasp. "No. I've lost my appetite."

She picked up her purse and speed-walked toward the exit. Chance threw a hundred-dollar bill down on the table before running behind her. He caught up with her as she waited outside the passenger door of his car. Her arms were folded as she waited for him to lock the door. She looked as if she could kill someone right now.

"Are you telling people that you broke up with me?" she asked.

He looked down and away, but April stood her ground. They were not leaving the parking lot until he answered.

"Not exactly."

"What the hell is that supposed to mean?"

"I've been under a lot of pressure to keep you out of the department's hair lately. Rocky knew it was causing a rift between us. In trying to look out for me, he told other people at the department that you and I were not seeing eye to eye. When I showed up at the ball without you, they just assumed it was true... and I let them."

"Wow. Take me home." She started to get in the car.

"Wait! Hold up, April," Chance barked. "Are you working with the firm right now?"

"Not exactly," she said as she sat down and closed the door.

Chance shoved Rocky into the open locker.

"Don't you ever disrespect April again!"

Rocky pushed him back.

"What do you expect? Her firm is trying to take away everything I have. How about you talk to your woman and get her to leave me the hell alone?"

"April has nothing to do with the investigation into the shooting, Roc. She's been on leave for months now. You got the wrong information, bro."

Rocky smirked. "She really has you wrapped around her finger, Chance! You really believe that her office attempting to bring charges has nothing to do with her?"

"I'm pretty sure she is not involved. But what does it matter? They won't have enough evidence to try you."

Rocky squared his shoulder and narrowed his eyes.

"Yeah, like Russo was found not guilty?" he shot back.

Chance shook his head.

"This is different, Roc. Russo had a long history of causing trouble and using excessive force. He was convicted because his attitude was fucked up."

Rocky laughed. "Exactly! What you think the jury would think about me?"

Both of the men fell silent.

"You won't be charged so there's no need to stress about what a jury will think."

Rocky turned away and slammed his locker before sidestepping him and heading for the door.

"Aye, Roc!" Chanced yelled behind him. "Remember what I said. Leave her alone."

"Yeah, yeah, yeah," he replied without breaking his stride. He lifted his hand above his head and gave Chance the middle finger.

"I talked to Rocky yesterday. He shouldn't bother you again."

April looked up from here computer. Chance was staring at her.

"Great. Thanks."

He put the box of cereal back into the cabinet and sat in the seat next to her at the dining room table.

April fixed her gaze on her screen.

After a couple of bites, Chance dropped the spoon into the bowl.

"How long are you going to act like this?"

"Act like what?" she asked.

"Come on, April! You know what you're doing. You're mad at me and you're ignoring me."

She closed the laptop and turned to face him.

"I'm not mad at all. I just recognize that we are working toward two different goals." She shrugged and turned to get up.

Chance swung her back around toward him.

"But we're not! We just have different ways of getting there. You are a prosecuting attorney. You can be outspoken whenever you feel like it. I'm not in a position to do that yet, but when I am, I will."

She rolled her eyes.

"Like you were so outspoken when Rocky came for me?"

Chance shifted his gaze downward.

"April, I would protect you with my life! You don't know everything about the situation with Rocky."

"I know enough. I know he shoots unarmed citizens. I know he plants evidence. I know he disrespects women and bullies people. That sum it up?"

Chance stood up and paced back and forth.

"That's all true. There's more to him than that, though. Things haven't been easy for him."

She gasped. "So because things haven't been easy, he can ruin other people's lives?"

"Of course not! I'm just saying he's not all bad."

April stood up, grabbed her laptop and headed for the exit.

"Hey!" Chance yelled.

"Yeah?"

"I love you, April."

She turned and kept walking.

"The grand jury decided not to indict Mr. Moretti." Charlotte screeched as soon as April answered.

"But how the hell did they come to that conclusion? There was more than enough circumstantial evidence to indict him!"

"The key word is *was*. The witnesses that say he confessed have reneged on their statements. The department is completely uncooperative. The thin blue line is holding strong. It's almost like they knew we were trying to charge him before we submitted the request."

April thought about the confrontation she and Rocky got into in the restaurant. He clearly knew he was under investigation. She hadn't even thought to warn Charlotte.

"I'm sorry, Char. We'll definitely have solid evidence to get him for planting evidence in Tariq's case."

They hung up the phone and April collapsed on the couch, exasperated. The sooner they got Rocky out of the department, the more lives they would save.

The phone was ringing and April ran over to grab it, expecting it to be Charlotte again. Instead it was Rahim.

"Hey. How are you?"

"Not good, April. We just got word that Officer Moretti won't be charged."

"Yeah, I heard earlier. I'm sorry. You know how hard these cases are to succeed in."

"They are difficult... for everyone but you. Had you been the prosecutor, there would have been a different outcome," he asserted.

April was quiet. She knew it was true. The case needed someone who believed in it with all of their heart and there was no one better than her to pursue it.

"I know," she admitted.

"I wasn't trying to guilt you, April," Rahim stressed. "I'm just saying that you're the best at what you do.

"Thank you," she uttered.

"Any way, I called because Our Lives Count has organized a protest in front of the police station tonight at eight and I wanted to see if you could attend."

April froze. This was the kind of event she should be participating in. She thought about Chance and what the consequences would be for him, but then thoughts of Rocky disrespecting her and then Chance and Candice Reynolds showing up to the Policeman's Ball arm-in-arm flashed in her head.

"I would be honored to attend. I'll see you there."

Next, she called Charlotte and Janice to let them know about the event and ask them to join her.

April could feel her knees knocking as she, Charlotte and Janice walked toward the growing crowd in front of the precinct. Everything seemed to be moving in slow motion. Her stomach was in knots and she felt nauseated.

"You alright, sis?" Janice asked with a concerned look on her face.

Unable to speak, April just nodded and smiled.

"Good. Isn't this exciting?"

Again April nodded and smiled. Excitement was not exactly what she was feeling right now. She wished the protest were not at Chance's precinct, but knew it was where the message would be most visible and disruptive.

They finally saw Rahim and made a beeline through the crowd to get to him.

"April! Thanks for coming!" He leaned in and hugged her. Instantly, she felt more comfortable.

"Thanks. Of course, you know my sister, Jan, and this is my partner at my firm, Charlotte."

He greeted both women, then started to explain what the evening would look like. April was relieved because she hadn't known what to expect.

"Hey, sis!"

April turned to see Tariq and his girl approaching.

"Tariq! What are you doing here? This isn't safe!"

"I understand that. But sometimes you gotta put fear aside and do what's right, you know?"

She immediately thought about how frightened and nervous she had been on her way here. If Tariq could risk his life to be here, a little drama at home wouldn't kill her.

"You're absolutely right, Tariq. I'm proud of you!"

They hugged and as soon as they let go, Janice handed each of them a sign.

The police marched out of the precinct in riot gear. They lined up on the landing between the building and the protestors with shields and batons and stared out over the crowd straight-faced. April swallowed hard when she noticed Chance taking his position in the middle of the line. She shrunk back toward the crowd in an effort to blend in. Then she noticed Rocky standing shoulder to shoulder with her man. A rush of anger came over her. Her chest tightened and she pushed her shoulders back, stepping forward once again.

"You alright, sis?" Jan whispered into her ear. Her forehead was wrinkled and she made sure she made eye contact with her sister.

"Huh? Yeah, I'm good," April smiled reassuringly.

Nevertheless, Jan placed a supportive hand in the small of her back.

The crowd had begun their signature mantra, OUR LIVES COUNT! OUR LIVES COUNT! OUR LIVES COUNT! At first, April just mouthed the words silently, but the vibration of the words and the emotion behind them proliferated the crowd of over one thousand people and suddenly, she felt like part of the movement. Her muffled tone escalated and before she knew it, April was shouting OUR LIVES COUNT! OUR LIVES COUNT! She looked to her left and right and saw that Charlotte and Janice had both gotten caught up in the energy of the crowd. They each held a sign high above their head, chanting in unison.

Despite the angst that was directed at him, Chance remained stoic. His face was expressionless and he stood holding onto his baton like a soldier ready for war. April felt sick. She asked herself what they had in common. As one of only a few brown faces on the force, he stuck out like a sore thumb. She looked around and noticed the entire of group of activists seemed to be directed at him. But could she blame them? She was engaged to the man and couldn't understand how he could stand there ready to land on the wrong side of history for a check.

Rocky, on the other hand, couldn't hide his acrimony. He wore a noticeable scowl on his face and even from this far away, she could see that he was holding his baton so tightly that his knuckles had turned white. He held it in one hand and pounded it into the other over and over.

The crowd had gotten so loud that nothing else could be heard. Their frustration was palpable and April wondered what was next. They had taken a few steps forward and so had the police. It seemed a confrontation was inevitable. Anxiousness overtook her. She wanted to let their voices be heard but didn't want anybody hurt in

119

the process. The police officers' body language had shifted and there was nowhere positive to go from here. April stepped forward and tapped Tariq on the shoulder. He leaned in so he could hear her.

"Should we go now?" she asked him.

Tariq frowned. "No. We're just getting started."

April clasped her hands together. "But Tariq, it's getting crazy out here! Somebody's gonna get hurt!"

He laughed giddily and placed one hand on each of her shoulders.

"That's what protest is about, April! This ain't the courtroom counselor. This is real life…"

With that he spun around and rushed to the front of the crowd to confront the police. April shook her head back and forth. She looked around for Char and Jan, but they had been swallowed in the mass of people.

She turned back toward the precinct and noticed Rahim standing a few feet away. She rushed over and tapped him on the shoulder. He stopped and faced her.

"Hey, April. What's up? You good?" he asked.

She cleared her throat. "Actually, I wanted to talk to you for a sec. The crowd is getting angry and the police are getting anxious. I'm worried about everyone here. Especially the women and children."

He gave her a concerned look.

"April, I understand why you would feel that way. I want you to understand that we all know what the possible outcomes may be before we show up. We know there's a possibility someone could get hurt, but that's a sacrifice we are all willing to make in order to stand up for what's right."

"I get that, Rahim. But what about the little kids?"

"We always make sure they are out of harm's way."

She started to point out that there were several children in the area, but Rahim whistled loudly and made a few subtle hand gestures. Several men in the crowd hustled every child, along with their mothers away. April watched as they all made a beeline back toward their vehicles. She breathed a sigh of relief as they all disappeared out of sight.

"Feel better?" Rahim asked.

He was so close that his voice in her ear startled her. She backed away.

"Um… yes, I do. But can we talk about how this will end?"

"I'm listening…"

"Well, I want to get the message across, but I also--" Her voice caught in her throat.

Chance's eyes looked as if they would burn a hole through her. In all of the chaos, she had hoped he wouldn't notice her. She wanted to duck down and scurry away, but it was too late. His eyes were squinted but his body was still. She flashed an apologetic grin, but his face didn't change.

Rahim waved his hand in front of April's face. It was as if he was invisible. She continued to look beyond him. He turned to follow her gaze and met eyes with Chance. The two men stood silently sizing each other up. April looked back and forth between the two. She knew something needed to be done before it was too late.

She grabbed Rahim by the arm. "Let's just disperse the crowd. I think we've gotten our message--"

He snatched his arm, from her grip, smirked at Chance and stepped forward, lifting the bullhorn to his mouth. April stood alone with her mouth gaped open.

"Everyone, please, silence!" Rahim yelled. Right on cue, the crowd stopped chanting. "I want to thank you for your willingness to do whatever it takes to make sure justice is served. While some people prefer to be justice warriors from the safety of their homes or office..." he glanced at April, "you are out here on the front lines, putting community before self."

April folded her arms across her chest and scowled at him.

He turned his attention back to the front. "We expect the boys in blue to protect each other, no matter how wrong they are. What we don't expect is our own brothers to put their families, friends and communities on the back burner for money and prestige."

April sighed. She willed Rahim to just stop speaking. Chance watched the other man in anticipation.

"Officer Chance Carrington..." Rahim started. "He grew up in this community, but he is not one of us. You see a black officer policing the community and believe we will finally get some understanding and cooperation from law enforcement. But Officer Carrington is not our kinfolk. He's what I refer to as skinfolk. He looks like you and me, but that's about it. His main objective is to further his career."

"Motherfucker," Rocky mumbled. He stepped forward, but Chance placed an arm in front of him.

122

"Chill out, Roc," he ordered.

"We can't let this guy disrespect you, bro," Rocky barked, leaning in.

Chance continued to look ahead, but retorted, "The media is here, there is a lot of publicity. We can't lose our cool."

Rocky stood at attention. "Fine."

April attempted pulling the bullhorn away from Rahim, but he slipped out of her reach. The crowd began to boo and point at Chance. He maintained his composure, but his eyes were glassy and downcast. Even from a hundred feet away, she should see that his breathing was labored. Her heart ached for him.

Suddenly, a man with the bottom half of his face covered in a bandana emerged from the crowd and threw a boulder through the front window of the precinct. He turned to run and April stood in his way. She wanted to ask him why he had escalated the situation, but he was trying to sidestep her. She reached up and snatched the bandana from his face. He stood stunned momentarily. His blue eyes flashed with fear. His skin was tanned and his overgrown blond beard was now exposed. He was definitely not a part of the Our Lives Matter movement.

"Hey! Who are you? Why did you do that?"

He shoved her to the ground and disappeared into the crowd.

Tariq ran over and lifted April back to a standing position. "You okay, sis? Was that a cop that pushed you down?"

Before she could answer, there was a loud thump as a baton came crashing down on the back of his head.

He fell forward, toppling April and landing on top of her. The weight of his body felt as if he had been knocked unconscious. She struggled to get out from under him. Everything seemed to be moving in slow motion as she looked up at the officers and the crowd embroiled in physical battle. She finally slid out from under Tariq and stood in front of him to keep him from being trampled. She yelled out for help, but Janice and Charlotte were still nowhere to be found. She looked around for Rahim and saw that Rocky had him in custody, leading him to a mobile holding cell.

"Arrest him!" An officer yelled, pointing at Tariq, who had regained consciousness and was sitting straight up. A couple of other officers rushed over.

April blocked their path. "He was knocked unconscious. He is no threat to you. Leave him alone!" She started shoving them away.

One of the officers raised his baton in the air and lunged toward her. She cowered, squeezed her eyes shut and raised her hands above her head to block. She braced herself for impact.

"What the hell are you doing, Carrington?" One of the officers shouted.

"What does it look like I'm doing? Back the hell up!"

April opened her eyes to find Chance standing inches from her, facing his cohorts. One of the officers leaned into his shoulder and said something inaudible on the radio. They backed away a few feet.

"Chance, thank you so much!" April exclaimed. She leaned in to hug him, but he placed a palm on her chest. She dropped her arms to her sides.

He walked around her and stood over Tariq. Her heart pounded hard and fast. Suddenly, Chance bent over and offered a hand to his childhood friend. At first, Tariq rejected the gesture and tried to get up on his own. When he wobbled and fell back to the ground, he finally took Chance's hand and was pulled to his feet.

"You alright?" Chance asked.

Tariq rubbed the knot on the back of his head and winced. "Yeah, I'm cool. Thanks." He walked off.

He looked at April and seemed to want to say something. She waited, hoping he would, but he just looked her up and down before turning away.

"Carrington!" the lieutenant boomed as he fast approached.

"Lieutenant?" Chance replied.

"What is going on here? I'm hearing that you're having a problem, handling the response to this situation?"

Chance shot a glance at the officers standing behind the lieutenant. They never did like him.

"No, sir. No problem at all."

"Good. I need you to step aside and let these officers take these rioters into custody."

"Rioters?" April shrieked. "There was no rioting our here! The Our Lives Matter movement was having a peaceful protest."

"Is that why the window to the precinct is shattered, Ms. Story?" the lieutenant asked.

"That was no one from this group. I saw the person myself!"

The lieutenant waived her off.

"Step aside, Carrington."

Chance stood erect. "No."

"Are you refusing a direct order?"

"With all due respect, sir, she's right. The agitator was not with this group and these people have done nothing wrong. My advice is that everyone stand down."

The lieutenant stepped toward Chance until he was almost nose to nose with him.

"Did I ask for your advice? I am giving you a direct order and expect you to comply."

April could see beads of sweat forming on Chance's forehead. His jaw clenched repeatedly and the beat of his pulse quickened in the vein running along the side of his neck. She placed a hand on the back of his shirted and tried to gently pull him away from the lieutenant, but he didn't budge.

"No can do, sir. This is my fiancée. She has done nothing wrong. There is no way I'm going to allow her to be taken into custody unjustly."

"You sure you want to do this?" the lieutenant pressed.

April stepped up next to Chance and held out her arms with her palms facing up.

"It's okay, Chance. I'll be out by tomorrow," she assured him. "Go ahead, officers, take me into custody."

Chance swatted her arms down and nudged her behind him.

"April, let me handle this. Like I said, there is no way I will allow my woman to be taken into custody. End of story."

"As you wish, Carrington. Meet me in my office after the area is cleared." With that he turned and motioned for the other officers to move along and walked away.

April gulped. She should have been relieved about the situation being de-escalated, but she knew that the repercussions were just beginning for Chance. He was still standing there, his chest heaving up and down as if he were trying to catch his breath. She placed one hand on his shoulder.

Chance spun around and grabbed her by her outstretched arm. She could feel him trembling slightly. His eyes were slits.

"April, go home!" he snarled.

She pulled her arm back, afraid to speak. Janice and Charlotte appeared out of nowhere.

"Hey, get your hands off my sister!" Jan screeched, pounding on Chance's chest. He stared down at her, unfazed.

"Jan, stop. He wasn't hurting me! Let's go." She grabbed both of the ladies by the hands and rushed away.

Janice shot him one last look of warning before they were out of sight. Several protesters had been arrested and the ones who hadn't were gone. Chance walked back toward the precinct. All of the other officers stood staring in his direction with disgust. He held his head high and his chest out refusing to be intimidated.

When he was entering the double doors, Rocky patted him on the back and nodded at him. He nodded back.

"What the hell was that all about?" Janice demanded once they were safely in the car.

April explained everything that had just happened to her and Charlotte. They were both oohed and aahed at every detail.

"Oh my God, sis! I hope Tariq and Rahim are okay. I have a little respect for Chance. What he did was big!"

"Janice, what he did just ruined his shot at Assistant Chief of Police! I really messed up." April cried.

"I'm so sorry this happened," Charlotte murmured as she massaged April's shoulders.

"Well, I'm not!" Janice spat. April's eyes widened and her head snapped in her sister's direction.

"What? I'm not. This is what standing up for what's right means! You put yourself and your desires on the back burner and do what's right. Besides, sis, how much longer could you go on loving a wimp who kisses up to the man and doesn't have your back? Today, in my eyes, Chance became a real man."

"He was always a real man!" April shot back.

The car fell silently. She stared out the window replaying what had went down. Never in a million years had she imagined Chance would stand up to his lieutenant on her behalf. The fact that his coming to her defense like her knight in shining armor felt good, but did nothing to quell the intense guilt she felt.

Janice pulled up in front of the house and let April out. She walked toward the door with her shoulders slumped.

"Hey, sis?"

April swung around. "Yeah?"

"Cheer up. Everything in the universe happens exactly as it should," Jan said before driving off.

CONSEQUENCES

Chance took a deep breath before knocking on the door. He tapped lightly.

"Come on in, Carrington," the lieutenant beckoned.

Chance slipped into the door and slid into the chair in front of the oversized cherry wood desk.

The lieutenant continued typing on his laptop for several minutes before looking up to address him.

"Sir, what's up?" Chance asked.

He pushed his laptop away and fixed his eyes on his subordinate.

"You do understand that there will be extreme repercussions for your actions this evening, right?" the lieutenant asked.

Chance cleared his throat. "Actually, I'm not sure why there would be an issue with anything I did. My job is to protect and serve. That's exactly what I did."

The lieutenant chuckled. "That is exactly what you did, isn't it? But you didn't protect your brothers in uniform. It seems to me that you were protecting your *homies from the hood,*" he said, using air quotes.

Chance could feel the heat rising under his collar.

"My *homies from the hood*?"

"You heard me, Carrington. I have gone to bat for you, giving you opportunities one of *you people* would never realize elsewhere."

130

Chance sat up and leaned forward. "You haven't given me shit! I'm the hardest working cop in this department. I have done everything asked of me without question. I have earned everything I have received!" His fists clenched, he pounded on the heavy desk.

The lieutenant leaned in. "Don't kid yourself, *brother.* Do you know how many good, clean officers that come from good backgrounds would love to be in your position? I think you need to work on your gratitude, boy!"

Chance leapt from his seat. He paced back and forth as he thought about wrapping his hands around the lieutenant's neck and choking the life out of him.

"Don't even think about it, Carrington. I'll have your black ass under the jail so fast, it'll make your head spin. By the way, my recommendation is off the table."

He willed himself toward the door, walked out and slammed it behind him. He stalked past his co-workers who all pretended to be busy doing other things. Rocky ran up next to him and tried to keep pace.

"Chance, you okay? What happened?"

"Not now, Roc," he said before exiting the double door and getting into his car.

April gulped down half the glass of wine and walked over to peek out the curtain for the umpteenth time. It had been a couple of hours since she got home and Chance had not showed. She called him several times only to be sent straight to voicemail. Calling the precinct was not an option.

Finally, the flash of headlights turned into the driveway. April leapt from the couch and swung open the front door. When Chance emerged from the car, his brows were drawn together, his jaw was taut and his nostrils flared. April had seen him upset on a few occasions, but this time was different. His hands were balled into fists at his sides and he brushed past her as if she weren't standing there.

Chance made a beeline to the kitchen, opened the bottle of Hennessy and poured himself a full glass. April had followed him, but remained silent as she watched him down the entire glass and pour another. He was deep in thought as he drank glass after glass. Every time she thought about saying something, his hardened expression made her think twice.

Chance had just sucked down his third glass of liquor and was about to pour a fourth. April walked over and placed her hand on top of his. He scowled at her, but beneath the anger, sadness clouded his features. He slowly pulled his hand back and went to have a seat at the dining room table. She sat next to him.

"Chance, I'm sorr--"

"Save it, April. You ain't sorry."

She forced a smile. "You have every right to feel that way. I am sorry, though. I had no intentions of putting you in that situation."

The chair squeaked across the hardwood floor as he stood up and started pacing.

"You have no fucking idea, what situation I'm in! Why couldn't you just trust me, April?" He threw his hands in the air and studied her, awaiting the answer.

Her hands formed a steeple and she tried to find the right words to say. The recognition that she hadn't trusted him shown on her face.

"I--I didn't trust you, Chance. I didn't trust you to stand up for what's right or to protect me." she admitted.

Tears filled his eyes.

"I had a plan, April. I was sacrificing to make real change in the end. How could you be with me if you didn't think I would protect you and thought I was too weak to stand up for what's right?"

She cast her eyes downward.

"I was wrong."

He leaned on the table and looked directly into her eyes.

"Do you know what it's like to be treated like less than a man because of your skin color? To be told you need to be grateful for opportunities that you worked hard to earn?" He pounded the table.

April startled but did not speak.

"I have worked for everything I have, but to my job, I'm still just a *homie from the hood*. I'm expected to go along to get along and if I decide to use my voice, I'm a problem. Do you know how difficult it is to stifle who you are just to be accepted by people who have no clue about what it means to be you?"

His voice tremored and his bottom lip quivered. The tears that had formed in his eyes now rolled uninhibited down his cheeks. April felt the wetness from her own tears trickle down her face and drip off of her chin.

Chance ran his hand over his face, willing the tears to stop. Angry at himself for allowing this to make him cry, he roared loudly. April jumped and leaned back away from him. He walked into the kitchen and picked up the glass he had been drinking from, slamming it into the wall. Crystal shattered onto the kitchen floor.

"Fuck it. Fuck the department. Fuck trying to prove to you that I am a man while you chase another man and get behind his cause. I'm done with all of this shit, April."

She stood up and rushed over to him.

"Please, Chance. Don't say that. I love you. Let me help you fix everything. I'm so sorry."

She wrapped her arms around his shoulders and to her surprise, he bent down, buried his face in the crook of her neck and wept. Again, she cried with him. He gripped the sides of her waist and kneaded her flesh hard, pulling her into him. In turn, she pressed the full length of her body firmly against his, gently massaging his head while she planted delicate kisses on the side of his neck.

Chance gripped the material of the long t-shirt she was wearing so hard; April was afraid it would rip. Her skin stung under the pressure of his tight grip, but she didn't stop him. In one quick scoop, he cupped his hands beneath her butt and lifted her up so she was eye to eye with him. Her legs seemed to have a mind of their own when they wrapped snugly around his waist.

She used her thumbs to wipe the tears from his face. He leaned in and nipped her bottom lip. Her lips separated involuntarily and he slid his tongue into her mouth. Her eyes rolled back and she let out a muffled moan. She could feel her center moisten against his rock hard abs. Now Chance began to devour her mouth. He sucked her tongue aggressively, pulling it in and out of his mouth over and over. He bit and slurped her lips, leaving them sore. She tried to match his pace, but it was no use. April just relaxed and let him have his way. Just when she thought her bottom lip would start to bleed at any moment, he pulled back, spun around and sat her on the kitchen counter with a thud.

"Ow... that hurt!"

"Good. You deserve it." he said, his eyes low and his voice deep.

She tried to kiss him, but he pushed her back against the cupboards. April furrowed her brows.

Chance yanked her t-shirt up over her head and tossed it to the floor. He then reached around her and unclasped her bra. She moved forward to make it easy for him. Her heart was racing and her chest heaved up and down. He palmed both of her breasts, massaging them deeply and brought his mouth in to taste them. He sucked hard on one of her nipples, then the other, seemingly unable to decide which one he wanted most. She threw her head back and arched her back. She ran her fingers over his waves, but he grabbed her hand and slammed it against the cabinet.

"Don't touch me," he warned.

He continued his assault on her breasts and she squirmed in pleasure trying to keep her hands off of him.

Finally, he released her and she squealed in protest. He stood straight up and studied her.

"You fucking with him?" he demanded.

Taken aback by the question, April sat up straight.

"With who? What are you talking about?"

He slammed the palm of his hand into the cabinet next to her head and she jumped.

"Don't play stupid, April. You know exactly who I'm talking about. You show up at *his* rally and stand by while he assassinates my character in front of the whole city."

"I swear, I had no idea that was going to happen, Chance! I was only there because I wanted to do something... anything to help. I have no interest in anyone but you."

He stood there, contemplating her words. She pleaded with her eyes, willing him to believe her.

"Good. You'd better not." he finally said.

He wrapped his hands behind her knees and slid her forward until her back fell flat on the counter, her head barely missing the cabinet. He grabbed the sides of her panties and ripped them from her body, causing her sweet spot to gush. He kneeled before her and planted his face there, lapping up her wetness and mimicking the assault he had inflicted on her mouth. April writhed in ecstasy, holding onto the counter for dear life. Every time she forgot the rules and tried to run her fingers over his head, he slapped her hands away and mumbled "don't touch me" into her box. When she finally orgasmed, he reached up and pinned both wrists down, continuing to lap her up and she jerked and screamed. Finally, he stood up and used his hand to wipe away the juices that dripped from his beard. April was spent and laid there shaking.

Chance pulled his own shirt over his head and unbuckled his belt. Even before he unleashed it, his thick shaft pressed against his dark blue trousers, begging to be freed. When he finally stepped out of his pants, it stood at attention. April sat up, her mouthwatering. She wanted to give it the same attention he had given hers. He pushed her back to a prone position. Before she could protest, he entered her causing a loud groan to escape her lips. He pumped and pounded, talking to her all the while.

"Next time I tell your ass to stick to the plan you do it."

"Okay... baby," she agreed in between whimpers.

"If I ever catch you following another man around, I'm going to fuck both you and him up."

"Yes, daddy."

It had been awhile since they were intimate and she could already feel her tight walls starting to swell. He could feel it, too, because it was becoming more and more difficult to speak. He moaned and grunted in response. The pleasure and pain was too much to bear. April exploded once again. Her wetness was all over him and he started to move faster and faster, in and out, out and in. He suddenly let out a guttural sound before squirting inside of her. His random movements continued until he had nothing left to give and collapsed on top of her.

Both of them laid there until they caught their breath. Then he slid out of her, picked her up and carried her to the bedroom where he held her as he drifted off to sleep. April stared at the ceiling feeling like despite everything, this would be a new start for her and Chance before closing her eyes.

The sound of doors and drawers slamming snapped April out of her comfortable sleep. She reached over her head and stretched without opening her eyes. Missing the warmth of Chance's body, she backed up toward his side of the bed. Feeling no contact from him, she reached back and felt for him with her hand. The cold, empty sheet met her and she let her eyes crack open. She scanned the empty room but saw no sign of Chance. April fell quiet and listened until she heard him shuffling around in the front of the house. A smile spread across her face. *He must have got up early to surprise me with breakfast.* She pried herself out of bed and made her way to the master bathroom. When she stepped inside the stall and turned on the shower, the hot water cascaded over her body and fogged up the mirror. She took her time and let it rinse away all of the drama from yesterday.

April threw on a sweat suit and her fuzzy slippers and walked out of the bedroom.

"Babeee?" she cooed as she shuffled through the living room toward the kitchen.

She scrunched her face up when he didn't respond. She entered the kitchen and frowned when she found that Chance was not there.

"Chance? You hear--" April froze in place.

Her mind couldn't process that black luggage set that had been placed at the front door. It seemed out of place. She glanced around the living room feeling as if something was amiss. The photo of Chance's mother had been removed from the montage on the wall leaving a blank spot that seemed to be shining bright. She swung her head toward the far wall and noticed that all of his awards and certifications were gone as well.

"Chance!" she yelled, all of the sugary sweetness gone from her voice."

"Yeah?" He stepped out of the guest bathroom with his shaving kit in his hand.

April waved her hand in the direction of the suitcases. "What's going on."

He took a deep breath and walked over to her. "Sit down. Let's talk."

She huffed and folded her arms. "I will not sit down. Just tell me what's up."

He threw his hands up in surrender. "Fine, April. A lot has happened recently and I need some space to think things through."

April scoffed. Chance tried to take her hand, but she pulled away.

"Why did you have sex with me last night? You knew you were leaving today."

He shook his head back and forth fast. "I made the decision this morning. Last night was emotional. I was acting off emotion," he shrugged.

Her eyes narrowed and she fought back tears. He had never treated her this way. She felt cheap. There was no way she was going to beg a man who wanted to be gone to stay.

"Okay, Chance. Good luck." She stepped aside clearing a path for him.

He tilted his head to the side. "Come on, April. It's not like that. I'm going through a lot. I just want to be alone to sort it out."

She swung around to face him and leveled a glowering look. Her finger wagged in his face. "You could have told me this before you laid up with me and saved me some fucking embarrassment."

"And you could have told me you would show up at my job with another man and humiliate me!" he snapped through gritted teeth.

She fell silent, but met his unrelenting stare. They held each other's gaze for what seemed like forever before he stomped past her, picked up his bags and whisked out the front door, leaving it wide open.

April watched as he flung his belongings into the trunk and backed out of the driveway. She rested one palm flat against the frame of the door and the other over her heart, reeling from the rejection. Her eyes were watery pools. She hollered into the wind before slamming the door shut and collapsing onto the couch. Her body seized and convulsed and she cried freely into the pillow.

Bzzzzzz… Bzzzzz… Bzzzzz.

April woke and looked around into the pitch black darkness. The only light in the room shined through the open shades from a luminescent street light and the illuminated screen of her cell phone. She grabbed the phone and hit the green icon.

"Tariq! How are you?"

"I'm good, April. Thanks for having Janice bail me out."

She breathed a sigh of relief. "You should have never been assaulted and arrested. I'm so sorry that happened to you."

"Psssst! I'm good, sis. That little hit wasn't shit."

She chuckled at his show of bravado. "It sure looked serious when you were lying on the ground unconscious."

They both laughed.

"Anyway, I just wanted you to know I'm good and say thank you. Rahim wants to talk to you."

"Tariq, no!"

Ignoring her objection, Rahim's baritone voice hummed through her phone.

"Ms. Story…"

She could feel her blood starting to boil. "What do you want, Rahim?"

He didn't respond immediately, stunned by her venom.

"Uh… I just wanted to make sure everything was alright with you."

She rolled her eyes. "Do you really? Because from where I sat, you intentionally started a problem with my fiancé in front of everybody."

"I have no idea why you are making this personal, April. I was there to take on the police department and that's what I did." The seduction in his voice had been replaced with condescension.

She simmered with anger. "Don't play stupid. You specifically targeted Chance because of your own ego. You knew exactly what would happen!"

He huffed. "Look, I have no--"

She hung up the phone, unwilling to go around in circles with him.

April rose from the couch and began switching on lights before heading to the kitchen.

I can't believe I slept all day. I am starving.

She made herself some steaming hot chamomile tea and ramen noodles. As she sat at the table, she scrolled through her phone to see what she had missed.

Charlotte had called several times and sent text messages asking her to call. She had one message from Chance.

"April, I'm sorry about how things went, but I have done nothing wrong. I will be at the hideaway until I figure things out."

Bitterness filled her. She texted back, "You've been running around with Candice Reynolds for months behind my back. Don't play innocent, Chance."

She sat staring at the phone, awaiting a reply. After ten minutes had passed, she gave up.

"April, I've been looking for you all day!" Charlotte screeched before the phone finished its first ring.

"I know, Char. I'm sorry. I literally slept all day."

Charlotte's tone changed. "Oh no, April. Is everything okay?"

April's eyes glistened and she pursed her lips. "Not really, but I'll fill you in later. Now what was so important today?"

"Oh! I have good news! We were able to retrieve that recording from Tariq's phone from the night he was arrested by Rocky and Chance."

Her heart sank. She had wanted to find evidence that Rocky set Tariq up, but has also known that doing so could implicate Chance. He had promised that he would never do such a thing, but she wasn't so sure. This recording was going to change what she thought about him forever.

"Okay. What does it show?" She held her breath, bracing for the truth.

"Exactly what Tariq said it would. He and Officer Moretti got into an altercation during the traffic stop. Officer Carrington separated them and spoke with Tariq at his window, while Officer Moretti returned to the patrol car. I am assuming he went into the trunk because you can hear it slam on the recording. He returns to Tariq's car and requests that his trunk be opened. He and Officer Carrington have a tense, muffled discussion about the search of the trunk. I couldn't make out everything, but it's apparent that they are not in agreeance. Finally, Moretti, hits something against the car and demands the trunk be opened. Tariq complies, Carrington returns to the window to tell him everything will be fine and voila! Officer Moretti finds two pounds of marijuana in the trunk."

April was stunned. She knew that Rocky was dirty, but to plant evidence that sent a man to jail? How could he live with himself?

"That's great news, Char. I am hoping it's enough to bring charges against him."

"But that's not all!" Charlotte shrieked gleefully.

"What, Char?"

"So, during that arrest, Tariq is saying it's not his. Rocky takes his phone, but it continues recording. He says *I know* to Tariq and laughs!"

April stood up and stomped her feet, gleefully.

"And, I have the evidence re-tested. It turns out that Moretti's fingerprints are all over the inside of the packages!"

"Oh my God, Char! We've got him! I'm coming in tomorrow morning to help you prepare the case."

"Will do, boss lady!"

April shook her head from side to side and sat back down. "No, Char, this was all you. I have been completely out of it and you made this happen. You did a great job."

"Thank you, April. I will see you in the morning."

"Wait! Char... What about Chance? Did he do anything wrong?" She sat wide-eyed waiting for the response.

"It doesn't seem that way. From what I heard, he was unaware of what his partner had done.

April exhaled. "Thank you. I will see you in the morning."

BETTER SAFE THAN SORRY

She sat on the couch with the phone in her hand. Chance had walked out on her, but there was no way she could let him hear about this from anywhere else first. April hesitantly dialed his number and listened as the phone rang. After several rings she started to hang up, but his voice blared through the handset.

"Hey, April," he greeted dryly.

She immediately regretted making the call. "Hi, Chance. Are you busy?"

"A little bit, but I have a sec. What's up?"

April inhaled deeply. "I need to tell you about something serious that's about to--"

She stopped mid-sentence. There was a woman in the background. It sounded as if she were having a conversation on another phone.

"Oh. Are you out and about?" April asked calmly.

"Nope, I'm exactly where I told you I would be." He sounded irritated.

She could feel her angering simmering. It took everything she had to keep from exploding. "So you have company at *our* place right now?"

"Look, April, just tell me what it is you have to say. I am working on something with Candice and need to get back to it."

She bowed her head and a flush crept over her face.

"April? You still there? What's going on?"

"Never mind, Chance. I shouldn't have called. Have a good night."

He tried to interject, but she hit the end button and flung the phone across the room. She marched into her room, grabbed a blanket and pillow and returned to the couch for a long night of tossing and turning.

"Wow, April. You look like something the cat drug in," Charlotte said matter-of-factly.

"Thanks, Char." she rolled her eyes. "I didn't get a wink of sleep last night."

Charlotte's eyelids drooped. "Oh, no. I'm sorry. Do you want to talk about it?"

"Not really. Let's get this case against Officer Moretti together."

She walked briskly toward her office with Charlotte in tow, rattling off everything she knew about the case. April sat down in her black leather office chair and clasped her hands together, listening intently.

After hearing all of the details, April went through a timeline of how they would proceed and set expectations. Charlotte agreed to compile the charging documents. She turned to leave.

"Before we take any action, I would like to let the Chief of Police know about the upcoming charges."

Charlotte stopped walking and turned to face April. Uncertainty shown all over her face.

"What is it?" April asked.

Charlotte shifted back and forth from one foot to the other. "I was just thinking... given the circumstances with you and Chance, it may be better to just do it without letting the department know."

April stood up and walked over to her. She took one her of Charlotte's hands and clasped both of hers around it. "Thank you so much for looking out for me. Everything will be fine, Char. We will give them the same professional courtesy we would give under any other circumstance. We can't let my personal relationship cloud our judgment."

Charlotte forced a smile and nodded affirmatively. She exited and headed toward her own office to make the call.

As April sat there scribbling down her arguments for the trial, she couldn't help but feel hopeful. She had never been a fan of Rocky's, but he was one of Chance's best friends. She was always worried that he would get Chance killed or fired or even arrested. It would be a relief to finally let the world know what kind of person he was.

Feeling satisfied with her game plan, April looked up and saw that it was already late in the afternoon. She grabbed her purse and overcoat and locked up her office before heading home for the day. When Charlotte saw her walking toward the front doors, she gave her a telling look that let her know she had reached out to the department about Rocky.

April drove down the busy street toward her house. She turned on Pandora and set it to the Beyoncé' station. *I'm A Survivor* blasted through the speakers and she sang along loudly feeling as if the words were her own. Deciding the traffic was too much to bear, she veered off onto a back street and started zigging and zagging toward her destination. Lost in the sounds of *Destiny's Child* and her own thoughts she didn't even notice that black Dodge Charger that had sped up behind her until it rammed the back of her car.

Her head slammed into the headrest first then impacted the steering wheel as she abruptly pressed the brake pedal all the way to the floor. Her phone went airborne and slammed into the windshield stopping the music she had been listening too. April felt dizzy, but could feel wetness running down her forehead. She gingerly touched her head and winced in pain. Her fingers were covered in blood. It was eerily quiet and everything seemed to be moving in slow motion.

Her stomach knotted when it dawned on her that she had been hit by another car. She whirled around to see if the driver had stopped. Fear hit her like icy water when the driver got out of the car and walked toward hers. He was tall and of a muscular build. His face was covered with a ski mask and he was dressed in all black. In his right hand, he held a handgun with what appeared to be a silencer on the end. Alarm rang in April's mind, but her body was paralyzed with fear. He walked with purpose as he approached her car; twenty feet away, fifteen feet away, ten feet away… he leveled the gun in front of him. April's body finally jumped into action. She gripped the steering wheel and punched the gas so hard, it felt like her foot would go through the floorboard.

The man ran alongside the car, trying to take aim at her until it got too far away from him. The sound of glass breaking rang in her ears as a bullet entered the back window and whizzed by her head. She swerved back and forth in case he continued to shoot, narrowly missing the parked cars lined up on the street. At the first cross street she came to, she swung a left, taking one last glance in the rearview mirror. The car was a block behind her and closing. Once she turned onto the main street, she glanced back once again. Instead of following, the assailant blew through the intersection and kept going. She tried to look for something to identify him, but his windows were blacked out. There was no way she could get a license plate number from this angle. April pulled into the parking lot at Dunkin' Donuts and dialed 9-1-1.

The officer took notes nonchalantly as she relayed what had happened.

He stopped writing and looked at her. "So let me get this straight. Some unknown guy follows you for some unknown reason, crashes into your car purposely and then tries to shoot you?" he chuckled. His partner turned away to keep from laughing.

Her blood was boiling. "That's exactly what happened. I could make a guess as to who did this to me, but your guess is probably as good as mine." She raised her eyebrows. It was clear that they would be of no assistance.

The officer narrowed his eyes at her. "Why do you need us? I'm sure you have a lot of *criminal friends* that could take care of this problem for you. I hear you all are good at that." He and his partner burst out laughing.

She gave them both a frosty look. "Are you going to do your job or do I need to get on the phone with your boss?"

They both doubled over in laughter again. "Call him! You really think anyone in law enforcement gives a damn what happens to you? I swear, you people get handed an opportunity to be in a position of power and instead being grateful, you start acting all uppity."

April's eyes shot at him. "You people? Who exactly are you referring to, Officer... Johnson?" she asked, leaning in to get a closer look at his badge.

Suddenly he grabbed her by the forearm. His grip was so tight; she could feel the blood circulation in her arm cutting off. Her skin burned as it pinched under his tight grip.

"Are you threatening an officer?" His sour breath blew right into her face.

Terror overtook her as she realized she was powerless. She looked around into the crowd of people who had stopped to look at the drama unfolding. She hoped that one of them would be brave enough to step forward and stop this blatant abuse of power, but no one seemed to want to be involved.

"Get your hands off of me!" She tried to pull her arm away, but there was no way she could overpower him.

"Now you're resisting arrest!" he yelled. His quiet partner bolted over to help. He grabbed April by the back of her hair and slammed her onto the hood of the car face first. Stars and flashes of light circled her head as the pain shot through her. Her forehead had stopped bleeding while she waited on the police. Now it reopened and blood gushed out, dripping all over the hood of the cruiser. Officer Johnson yanked her arms back and snapped handcuffs around her wrists while his partner held his hand on the back of her head forcing her face into the cold, hard metal. Her arms had been lifted so high in the air behind her, she felt as if they would snap right off of her shoulders. Her eyes flooded with tears. She tried to hold them back, but they fell on the hood of the car, diluting the blood smears already there. She cried out for help, but nobody seemed to care.

"Let her go!" the voice came from behind. April was still bent over the car and couldn't see who had demanded her release.

Officer Johnson dropped her wrists and turned his attention to the woman yelling at him. His partner let her head go and turned around, placing one hand on his baton and the other on his weapon. April stood up slowly and turned to see who it was that spoke up.

The woman was in her early twenties, slightly built and wore a hijab on her head. She was covered from head to toe in a burka and stood stone-faced as the officers approached. She held up a cell phone, pointing it directly at them. April's heart dropped when she noticed the small child holding onto his mother's hand. He squeezed close to his mother seemingly aware of the danger in this situation.

"Are you recording us?" Officer Johnson demanded.

"I am," the young woman said without hesitation.

His face turned crimson and he snatched his baton from his waistband.

"No!" April yelled. "It's okay, Miss." She scampered over and stood next to the officers, who no longer seemed to care about arresting her.

"Give me the phone, or you'll be going to jail, too!" he ordered.

The woman stood defiant. "This is my property and I am filming on public property. You have no right to confiscate my phone or put your hands on me." Her demeanor was eerily calm.

"Wait! It's okay. Here take me in." She turned away from Officer Johnson and offered him her cuffed wrists. She gave the young woman a pleading look. "I'll be fine. It's okay."

The woman stood stoic, her arm raised and the cell phone still recording every second of it. "No, it's not okay, sister. You have a right to be treated fairly by the people we employ. You have done nothing wrong and I refuse to stand by like these cowards and watch it happen," she gestured toward everyone gathered nearby.

As if her words had jolted them into action, several men stepped forward and got between the officers and the young woman and began to verbally protest the cops' actions.

Officer Johnson scowled. His partner glanced from one pedestrian to another, his hands trembling, but still resting on his baton and service weapon. Unwilling to take on the entire crowd, Officer Johnson jerked April by the chain that held her handcuffs together. She wretched in pain as she tripped and fell to the ground. He began to drag her back toward his cruiser. Several men now ran up on him and demanded that he release her. He began barking orders and swinging his baton with his free hand. His partner unholstered his service weapon and took aim at the men.

April couldn't move. She was paralyzed with fear about what the outcome to this situation would be. She squeezed her eyes closed and shook as she anticipated a gunshot. Suddenly the loud blare of sirens screamed into her ears. She slowly opened her eyes to see another officer speed into the parking lot. She looked up and thanked God when she saw Chance step out of the car.

He rushed over with a look of concern on his face. His expression turned to anger when he saw April on the ground at Officer Johnson's feet. He ran over and pushed him out of the way, lifting April to her feet. Sadness clouded his features when he took a close look at the injuries to her face.

"Oh my God. Are you okay, April?" he asked.

She wanted to say yes, but couldn't get the words out. She began sobbing as tears streamed down her cheeks. Chance pulled her in and held her. It was if the world stood still for a moment. The anxious crowd watched in awe and Chance's fellow officers seethed about his interjection but just stood there.

He finally released April and turned to them. "What the hell is going on here?"

Johnson stepped forward. "I should be asking you the same thing, Carrington. This was our call. What are you doing here? We have the situation under control."

Chance got right in his face. "Clearly, you don't have this under control. Several citizens called to report officers beating up a woman who called to report a robbery."

Johnson rolled his eyes and laughed. "I don't even think she was robbed. We were questioning her and she began assaulting me."

"That's a lie. I recorded the whole thing!" The young woman stepped forward, still holding her phone in one hand and her child's hand in the other.

Chance nodded in her direction. "Thank you, Miss. If possible, please keep recording.

The color drained from Johnson's face. "Moretti was right. You will do anything to protect your *baby mama!*" He threw up air quotes and began to laugh uncontrollably. He looked at his partner and he chuckled nervously.

BOOM! In one quick swoop, Chance had lifted Johnson from his feet and slammed him onto the hood of the car. Johnson's partner turned his weapon in their direction, uncertain of what to do. Chance placed a hand around Johnson's throat before turning toward the armed man.

"I suggest you holster your weapon... unless you're willing to go to jail for the rest of your life and throw your whole career away."

The officer seemed to give it some thought before slipping the gun back into his waistband. He slunk back toward the crowd and suddenly became a spectator.

"Are you finished?" Chance asked Johnson, who was gasping for air and trying to claw the hand off his throat. Chance softened his grip to give him an opportunity to answer.

"Yes!" Johnson blurted.

"Good." Chance snatched the keys from Johnson's belt and let him up. He rushed over and uncuffed April before turning back to his peers. "Both of you need to get to the station now. I will meet you there." He tossed the keys back.

Johnson mumbled something under his breath about Chance not being in charge, but hopped into his patrol car and drove in the direction of the station.

April leaned against Chance's car, taking in all that had happened today. He walked over and wrapped his arms around her once again. The crowd of people began to cheer. As if he had just noticed them, Chance let her go and addressed the crowd asking them to disperse.

The young woman walked over. "I want to make sure you get my recording, sir."

"Of course," Chance nodded. "I need to take her to the hospital and then the station. Can you follow us?"

"I didn't drive. My son and I were headed to the bus stop."

"Take my car and follow us," April finally spoke.

Chance's eyes widened. He leaned in to tell April what a bad idea it would be to give a stranger the keys to her car.

She put a hand up to stop him before he spoke. "I trust her. When no one else stood up for me, she did. I trust her." April and the young woman's eyes met and they held each other's gaze for some time before she took the keys and got into April's car to follow them.

INCOGNITO

"Follow up in a couple of weeks to get the stitches removed. Ice the bruises and wounds. Get some rest," the doctor said as he exited the room.

April stared down at her black and blue wrists. She could still feel the pain from the officer twisting her arms behind her back.

"I've gotta go. You good?" Chance suddenly blurted out.

April snapped out of her trance and looked up at him. Something about him was different. His small crow's feet had gotten a little deeper and despite all of the drama going on around them, he seemed to have a confidence and strength she had never seen in him. His presence made her feel safe and she really wanted him to stay.

"I'm good." She lied.

"Cool. I'll write up a report on everything that happened and let you know if I need anything additional." His tone was more clinical than the pristine white examination room they sat in. He turned to leave.

"Chance?"

"Yes," he replied without turning around.

"Thank you," April muttered.

"No problem. Just doing my job," Chance replied before rushing out the door.

She sat there feeling more alone than she ever had. Chance had just stepped on the toes of more officers and her anxiety about what might happen to him made her nauseous. She had asked for this; for him to stand up for what was right. Now that he had done it, April finally understood why it was so hard. She wished she could go back to listen and understand before things had progressed to this point.

The door swung open and Janice rushed into the room. "Oh my goodness! Are you okay, sis?"

April hugged her. "I'm fine, Jan. I will be okay."

Janice stood up with her hand on her hip. "Who the hell did this to you? It was that asshole, Rocky, right?"

She nodded.

"Well, there is no way you're staying at your house by yourself. You're coming with me to mom and dad's."

"You didn't tell them about this, did you? I don't want to worry them."

"Of course not. I wanted to see what was going on first. We're going to have to let them know, April. They can't be left in the dark about this."

"I know," April agreed.

Janice leaned in and hugged her once again. She suddenly stood up straight, just noticing the young woman and the child sitting quietly in the corner of the examination room. Her expression hardened and she stood in between the strangers and her sister.

"Who the hell is this?"

"Oh, Jan, this is--" before she could finish her introduction, the exam room door burst open again.

Tariq rushed in with Rahim behind him. He ran over and took her hand.

"April, you alright? I just heard about what happened."

She squeezed her old friends hand. "I'll be fine. Just a few bumps and bruises."

Rahim walked over hesitantly, not knowing what her reaction would be.

"Ms. Story…" he greeted softly.

"Mr. Salek," She retorted.

"I hope I'm not intruding. I heard about the incident and wanted to be here to support you."

Her features softened. She needed all of the friendly faces around that she could get right now.

"Thank you. I appreciate that."

Everyone was momentarily silent as they processed what had happened.

April decided to break the ice.

"Hey! Let me introduce you all to my new friend." She gestured toward the woman in the corner of the room. "This is Fatima Syed and her son, Mohammed. She was the first person that stood up for me today."

Everyone turned their attention to her. Despite her petite and unassuming build, her persona seemed larger than life. She acknowledged everyone as they introduced themselves and her son did the same. Rahim was particularly intrigued.

"It's very nice to meet you, Fatima." He moved in for a closer look. "Were you or your son injured?"

"We were not."

He breathed a sigh of relief. "Thank goodness. It's just not safe for you to intervene in these situations while your child is with you."

Her smile faded and she held his gaze defiantly. "I am very surprised to hear you say those words, Mr. Salek. If not me, who? And with all due respect, my son's life is in danger every day simply based upon the color of his skin. I have taught him since birth to stand up for what he believes in no matter the outcome."

Rahim's concerned look gave way to admiration. He and the woman locked eyes, neither of them speaking.

"I like her!" Janice exclaimed as she ran over and gathered her and her son into a tight group hug.

They all laughed.

"Have a seat, Carrington," the lieutenant ordered as soon as Chance walked into his office.

"Yes, sir." He planted himself on the hard leather chair prepared to hear his fate.

For what seemed like forever, the lieutenant continued to write. Chance sat patiently, not wanting to be the first to speak.

Finally, the man laid his pen down and narrowed his eyes looking directly at him.

"So, let me get this straight. You took it upon yourself to show up on another officer's scene, undermine him and interfere in an arrest?"

"An unjustified arrest," Chance added.

The lieutenant threw his head back and ran his fingers through his hair. His jaw tightened.

"Carrington, it seems you are letting your personal relationship bleed into your professional life."

Chance became heated. "With all due respect, that's bullshit, sir."

Lt. Grayson straightened his back and his eyebrows drew together. "Really? What makes you think you can show up whenever and wherever you want causing chaos?"

Chance slid the chair back and stood up. He rested both hands on the desk and bent forward into Lt. Grayson's face.

"The chaos was happening before I even got there. The officers were way out of line. We show up on scenes that we were not called to all the time. The only problem with this one is that I did what was right instead of letting them run rogue." He was starting to sweat. "So to answer your question, I give me the right to do the right thing whenever and wherever necessary!"

The lieutenant fumed. He, too, stood up and took the same stance that Chance had taken.

"It seems like you're ready to throw your whole career away over a nappy-headed hood rat."

Without thinking, Chance swung hard, connecting with Lt. Grayson's jaw. The man stumbled and struggled to stay upright, knocking everything off of his desk. When he finally regained his balance, he picked up his desk phone and started to dial.

He glared at Chance. "You're going to regret this, Carrington."

Chance smirked. "So will you, lieutenant. Go ahead. Make the call. I know where all the bodies are buried in this department. I'll burn this whole shit down!"

Lt. Grayson's eyes widened and he hesitantly returned the phone to its receiver. His office door opened and Rocky stood in the doorway, ready for action.

"Is everything okay in here, sir?" he asked the lieutenant, doing his best to avoid eye contact with Chance.

Lt. Grayson pulled a Kleenex from the box that was tipped over on his desk. He wiped the blood trailing from his nose and bottom lip.

"I'm fine, Moretti. I'll update you later."

Chance shot the lieutenant one last look of warning before turning to leave. Rocky squeezed to the side of the door to let him pass, but Chance grabbed two handfuls of his uniform and slammed him hard into the wall.

"Stay the fuck away from April or I will kill you! You understand me?"

"Bro, I don't know--" Rocky started.

Chance didn't let him finish. He pulled him in and then back into the wall even harder. "Do you understand me?"

Rocky nodded affirmatively and Chance released his grip and stormed out of the station. The entire precinct watched, stunned as he exited.

"I don't like this at all," Mrs. Story muttered while wringing her hands.

Janice rolled her eyes. "Mom, none of us like it, but it's happening. We just have keep April safe and make sure Rocky and his little friends in blue pay for what they did.

Her words did little to calm her mother. She continued pacing back and forth until Mr. Story walked in and wrapped her in his arms.

"Don't worry about a thing, honey. I will make sure everything is just fine." He kissed her softly on the temple and she relaxed into his arms.

April watched her parents. She had always been the one they never had to worry about. The fact that everyone was stressed about a situation she had brought upon them was almost too much to bear. Her head throbbed.

"I'm very concerned about Chance," Mr. Story offered, his forehead wrinkled. "That young man stood up for what is right and I'm afraid them white boys are gonna make him pay the price."

April heart jumped into her throat. The tears she had been holding back now escaped. Janice hurried over and sat by her.

"Chance is going to be fine, y'all. He knows how to handle himself. He's been navigating in the good ol' boys club for a long time now. He'll be okay." Janice assured her worried family.

Her words belied the angst she felt. She knew what happened to black men who didn't toe the line in their organizations. She had spent so much time believing that Chance was a sellout who would go along to get along. Now she was starting to wish she had been right about him. His actions of late would definitely put a target on his back.

April sat in the family room with the television on, but the volume muted. She had called and texted Chance numerous times and still had not received a response. With every minute that passed, she was getting more anxious. Finally, her phone rang and his name flashed across the screen.

"Chance! I was so worried about you! Are you okay?"

He paused for several seconds before answering. "I'm fine."

She waited for him to say something else; anything else, but the line was dead silent.

"What happened after you left the hospital? Did you go back to the station? How did everyone there react?"

He sighed. "I'm not in the mood to discuss that, April. I'm good though."

"Okay. You don't sound okay…"

"Look, I told you that I'm fine. Why can't you just listen? You always have to keep pressing and pushing! That's why we are where we are!" he barked.

She sat there stunned, uncertain of what to say. It was rare that Chance seemed to be at his wits end. She racked her brain to figure out the best thing to say next. Before she came up with anything he spoke.

"I gotta go. You stay safe."

The call ended and she sat there staring at the phone. She had hoped that speaking with him would make her feel better. Instead, her mind raced. *What happened to him? Why did he talk to me like that?*

There was no way she would get a wink of sleep. His words, "You stay safe" rang in her head over and over. At every creak of the house or gust of the wind she was up looking out the windows and checking the locks. She would need to get out of her parents' home as soon as possible. There was no way she was going to endanger them with her choices.

Tariq looked around cautiously. Since he had filed his case against the police department he had been on pins and needles. When they attacked him at the protest, he knew it wasn't safe for him in public. The latest incident involving April should have made him more worried, but instead it lit a fire under him. He was tired of being holed up in Rahim's place hiding out. He had decided he wasn't a prisoner and he'd be damned if he let them treat him like one.

Tariq pulled into the parking lot of one of his favorite hole-in-the-wall bars. The Hook, Line & Sinker had been a staple in his community for as long as he could remember. Everybody from the hood stopped by here from time to time to reconnect with old friends or drown their sorrows in a few shots poured by the heavy-handed bartenders.

"Tariq!" The petite Asian lady with the fiery red hair shrieked from behind the bar. "Where have you been?"

He smiled at her. "I've been out the way. How you been?"

She started to run down everything that had happened in the spot since he had last been there. They both laughed at all the drama that went down in the hood on a regular basis. The conversation took a sobering turn with she let him know that several officers had stopped by looking for him last week.

What makes them think they can come up on my stomping grounds to mess with me? He took one more glance around before getting comfortable.

"So, what'll it be?"

"Give me a double shot of Grey Goose."

The woman gave him a skeptical eye, but poured the drink anyway. When she slid it across the table, he gulped it down quickly and passed it back across the bar, silently asking her to refill the glass. She shook her head back and forth, but obliged his request. The woman turned to hand him the drink and stopped dead in her tracks. Tariq followed her eyes to the doorway. To his surprise, Chance walked in. He was out of uniform, but his demeanor gave his position as a cop away. He was preoccupied with his phone and looking down as he approached the bar. Tariq turned his stool toward Chance and planted his feet firmly on the sticky floor, prepared for whatever was about to go down. Chance was only a few feet from him when he finally looked up and noticed his former friend staring him down. He stopped walking and jerked back to put some distance between the two.

"Uh-- What's up, Tariq?" he stammered. "Surprised to see you here."

Tariq scowled. "You shouldn't be that surprised. You and your boys been in and out of here looking for me."

Chance shifted his weight under the speculative stares of everyone in the establishment. "I know nothing about that. It has nothing to do with me."

Tariq smirked. "Is that right? Then what are you doing here, Chance?"

Chance's expression closed up and his eyes shifted. He walked over and pulled out a stool a seat away from Tariq. "Same thing you're doing… having a drink."

The two men sat silently sipping on straight liquor and lost in their thoughts. After some time, Chance swiveled his stool to face Tariq.

"Listen, bro. I just want you to know that I'm sorry about what happened. You didn't deserve to go to prison."

Tariq bucked his eyes. He couldn't believe what he was hearing. "Now you apologize? Your partner ruined my life and you vouched for him! My family abandoned me. I lost everything." His eyes glistened and his jaw quivered as he spoke.

Chance's grabbed a napkin from the counter and dabbed the corners of his own eyes. "I know. I was wrong. I was selfish. I was too weak to stand up for what was right. You paid the price for it and I'm sorry."

Tariq was speechless. He wanted to be angry, but he could look into Chance's eyes and see the guilty eating away at him.

"Is that why you stood up for me at the protest."

He shook his head. "Nah. I did that because it was the right thing and you are-- were my friend. Everything, I've done since then is to make up for all the times I just let shit happen."

Tariq felt a sorrow that he did not want to feel for Chance. He had wanted an apology from him for years and now that he had it, he knew that it came at a price. In order to do what's right, Chance would need to put himself in danger.

Tariq threw a couple of twenties on the bar and walked toward the door.

"Aye, Tariq?" Chance yelled after him.

"Yeah?"

"Be careful, bro."

"You, too."

"I'll be fine, mom! You and dad just enjoy your vacation. I'll let you know when everything has blown over." She hung up.

April walked up to the door and was greeted by a security guard who towered over her and looked as if he could easily bend a car in half with his bare hands.

"We were expecting you, Ms. Story," he greeted as he stepped aside and let her into the heavy steel door.

She was lead down a maze of hallways and through another reinforced door before she stepped into the living quarters. The space was colorfully decorated and the walls bore paintings created by various artists. The famous figures depicted included Malcolm X, Martin Luther King, Jr., Nelson, Mandela and Maya Angelou, among many others.

Fatima and her son were the first to greet her. April wasn't surprised to see them here. It was evident that she and Rahim had made a connection at the hospital. The women hugged and April kissed the little boy on the cheek. Rahim and Tariq came out next, both excited to have her there and confident that they would all be safe.

"Let me show you to your room." Tariq grabbed her bags and led her down a nearby hallway, past an immaculate kitchen and to her temporary quarters.

April stepped into the room and looked around, there was a queen-sized bed, neatly made with a fluffy comforter. An overstuffed armchair sat in the corner near a lamp. The area seemed perfect for reading. A 32-inch television was mounted on the far wall and a desk, complete with a keyboard and monitor sat on the other side of the room. Her stay would certainly be comfortable.

Tariq stood there, watching her survey the room. Something in his stance told her he was aching to say something.

"What's up, Tariq?"

His eyes darted all around the room. "What you mean? Nothing."

April stepped over and got into his face. He continued to look all around him, avoiding eye contact.

"Don't lie to me. You know I can tell when you're not telling the truth, so don't even try it." She pointed a warning finger in his face.

Realizing that she wasn't going to take no for an answer, he sat at the foot of the bed, this time looking at her.

"What's up with you and Chance?" he started.

Her face twisted up. "I don't know. It's kind of complicated right now. Why?"

Ignoring her, he continued his line of questioning. "I know, but do you think y'all will be able to get back together? What happened?"

April moaned as she sat down next to Tariq slowly. "We just had two totally different ideas about serious issues… at least I thought we did. We couldn't agree."

He stroked his beard. "That's crazy. Y'all both always had each other's back."

She fidgeted with the ring on her finger. "I know. He had my back. I just didn't have his when it counted." The revelation hit her like a ton of bricks and she felt a cloud of darkness cover her.

Tariq put his head in his hands.

"What's going on, Tariq. Why are you asking me these questions?" Now her sorrow had become fear.

"Yesterday, I stopped by the Hook, Line & Sinker and I ran into Chance."

Her fists balled up in her lap. "Wow! Here I was thinking he had changed and he shows up there looking for you? I guess his priority is saving face for--"

Tariq put his hand up. "No, April. It wasn't like that. He wasn't there looking for me."

"Then what the hell did he want?"

"Nothing."

She laughed. "Oh, trust me, he wanted something!"

"No. He didn't even know I was there. He literally came in to have a drink. No uniform. No partners. No weapons. Just him."

They both stiffened. Chance had been the closest person to April for the last four years. He and Tariq went back as far as either could remember. He had gone to great lengths to distance himself from anything and anyone he thought would place him in a negative light among his professional peers. The fact that he had come there off duty was a serious sign that something wasn't right. They both knew it. She thought about calling him, but had already been blowing his phone up for the past couple of days to no avail.

"One other thing," Tariq muttered. "He apologized to me."

April's jaw dropped. "No… why?"

"He said he was wrong and he was sorry. I believed him, sis."

Her breaths quickened and her palms felt clammy. She wanted to see her fiancé and hug him. He had finally stood up for what was right and she wasn't there to help him deal with the consequences. She had thought about driving by the place he was staying multiple times, but didn't want to be clingy. At this point all of her pride went out the door. She stood up and headed toward the door. Tariq looked after her, bewildered.

"Wait! Where you going? You can't leave. It's not safe, April."

Before she could respond, her phone started ringing. She didn't recognize the number, but answered anyway.

"This is Charlotte!" Her voice was raspy and tearful.

"Char! What's wrong?"

"I'm downtown. I've been brought in for questioning," she whimpered.

April stopped in her tracks. "For what?" She exploded.

"I don't know. I was at the office working late and the police kicked in the door, claiming they had a search warrant. They were asking about drugs and money laundering... tore up the entire office and confiscated most of the files."

She slapped her hand over her mouth and leaned against the wall to steady herself. "Did they hurt you, Charlotte?"

"Nothing major. I took care of everything yesterday morning like you asked."

April didn't realize she had been holding her breath until she exhaled. "Thank goodness. I'm coming down to pick you--"

"No!" she blared. "Not you. Anybody but you."

She took the hint immediately. "Okay, Char. Sit tight. Somebody will pick you up shortly."

"I will not just sit here and wait!" April bellowed as she followed closely behind Rahim.

"He's right! They are obviously after you and your showing up in the station is exactly what they want," Tariq echoed.

"And your showing up at the station is safe? Last I checked they were after you, too, Tariq!"

"I understand. But I'm a man and--"

Her glare cut into him so hard, he knew he was definitely taking the wrong approach.

Tariq knew that arguing with April would be fruitless. "Come on!" He waved for her to follow them and rushed toward the underground parking garage.

The parking lot underneath was as big as the entire building above. On one side, there were various cars and SUVs and on the other, about ten Chevy Tahoes, all black with tinted windows. Rahim got into the back seat of one car, while Tariq and April were ushered into the back of another. A driver and a security guard slipped behind the wheel of each and three other drivers started the engines of three other lookalike cars. The caravan exited the structure and followed one another for several miles before arriving at the precinct.

April and Tariq sat tight while Rahim got out and entered the station, flocked by his security. Neither of them said a word as they waited on him to come out with Charlotte. After ten minutes, a familiar car pulled up and parked. Chance got out and walked toward the precinct. April reached for the door handle, but Tariq placed his hand over hers to stop him.

"I need to talk to him, Riq," she pleaded.

He didn't say a word, but nodded in Chance's direction. Her blood boiled when the car that had tried to run her off the road pulled up and parked near his. The fact that any damage it may have sustained when it rammed into her vehicle had magically disappeared made her want to vomit. She watched intently as Rocky climbed out of the driver's seat and made his way to the station. Chance seemed to be unaware of Rocky's presence and he looked at his phone while approaching the entrance.

"What are they doing here at night?" Tariq asked. "I thought both of them were on days."

"So did I..." April mused as she watched curiously.

Just as Chance was about to enter, Rahim's security guard burst out the front doors of the station with him and Charlotte in tow. Chance stopped and looked at them with a befuddled disposition. Although they couldn't hear the conversation, it was apparent that he was asking Charlotte why she was there. She started to explain, but Rahim stepped in front of her and said something to Chance, who appeared to be disputing that he was involved in what was going on. Rocky walked up and everyone, including Chance seemed startled by his presence. He smiled at Charlotte and must have uttered something distasteful because Rahim leapt in his direction. He came forward, welcoming a fight, but Chance stepped in between the two men. He turned around and admonished Rocky before ordering him into the station. Rahim, Charlotte and the security guards made their way toward the cars with Chance following closely behind. Now they could hear him asking questions about the search and inquiring about April. When they got close enough, she rolled her window down and made eye contact with him.

He rushed over and leaned near the window, peering inside. "Are you okay, ba-- April?" he asked.

"I'm fine. I wasn't there when this happened."

A look of relief washed over his face. "Good. I'm sorry this happened. I'm going to get to the bottom of it."

She nodded. "Thanks."

He started to walk away.

"Chance? Why are you here right now?" she asked.

He walked back over and looked around as if what he had to say was top secret. "I've been reassigned to night shift."

"Why? You hate working nights."

"Exactly. I'm persona non grata around here these days."

She reached through the open window and put a hand on his face. He closed his eyes, savoring the feeling of her warm palm against his cheek."

"I'm so sorry about everything. I should have listened to you. This is my fault."

His eyes popped open. "Yes, you should have listened. But this is not your fault, April. I should have also listened to you." He pulled her hand from his face, kissed it tenderly and let go. "You get back to safety." He looked over at Tariq. "Watch out for my girl."

Tariq nodded. "I got her, bro."

April wanted to stop Chance as he walked into the station. Instead she rode off into the night.

INTUITION

"You have to chill out, April," Charlotte warned. "Stressing yourself out about the situation will not change anything.

"She's right," Janice chimed in. Both ladies watched her pace back and forth.

"You just don't get it. Something isn't right with Chance. I can feel it. I'm so worried about him and I can't shake it."

Janice's face looked sorrowful. *Maybe I shouldn't have been so hard on him,* she thought. They had all wanted him to stand up against the wrong that was going on within his police department, but no one could have guessed things would turn out like this. "I know, sis. Everything's gonna be fine."

Fatima sat in the corner quietly. She hadn't said a word, but kept checking her phone to see if Rahim had called. After dropping April and Charlotte of at his place, he and Tariq had run back out in a hurry, saying they had business to handle. Janice had arrived shortly after. Now all the women sat anxiously waiting to hear from them.

Chance drove up and down the dark city streets on patrol. The town was pretty quiet this time of night, save for the occasional meth head here or there. That was exactly why he hated graveyard shift. The lack of activity made the hours drag on. If he were still partnered with

175

Rocky, at least he would have company, but tonight it was just him riding solo through the sleepy town.

"Patrol 5, standby." The dispatch blared through his radio.

He perked up, excited to have something to do. He had been ten minutes of boredom away from stopping for a coffee and donut in stereotypical cop fashion. He had also toyed with the idea of calling April, but knew it would be a mistake. Until this whole mess was cleared up, there was no way he would put her in more danger by getting close.

"Patrol 5, we have a 10-33 at 561 E. Union St. Please respond."

"10-4. I'm en route," he confirmed.

He made a U-turn, headed in the direction of the alarm. When Chance pulled up in front of the building, he immediately noticed that the street lights in the area were out. The alarm system was so loud he could barely hear himself think.

"Dispatch, advise that alarm company that I am on the scene and to disarm the alarm."

A few moments later, the sound stopped. Chance stepped out of his car and looked around. Save for the red, white and blue flashing lights on top of his car, everything was pitch black. He had turned his siren off, but the silence felt even more eerie. He shined his tactical lights on the entrance to the building. The front door was wide open and appeared to have been kicked off the hinges. He drew his service weapon with one hand and held his flashlight in the same direction with the other.

"Come out of the building with your hands up. This is the police."

He waited, but heard nothing. He inhaled and exhaled slowly, hoped to quiet the loud thumping of his heart. He swung to the left, believing he had seen movement in the shadows. Nothing there.

"Dispatch, I have obvious signs of a forced entry. Send backup. Over."

"Over," the dispatcher confirmed.

Chance continued through the front door of the building. He shined the flashlight all around the room and noticed cobwebs covering all of the furnishings. It smelled musty and there was a blanket of dust covering everything.

Who the hell would want to break into this place? He asked himself. He came upon a light switch and flipped it, but it didn't work. Inching further inside he repeated his warning and still received no response. As he inched toward the middle of the room he swore he saw something to his right; he shined the light and drew down, but there was no one there. His pulse quickened when he saw the cloud of dust they had left behind swirling in the beam of his light.

"Step out and show me your hands!" he yelled.

Suddenly, he saw a red dot out of the corner of his eye. He looked down to see the laser beam trained on his chest. Before he could react, a bullet whizzed through the air and struck him dead center on his torso. The wind was knocked out of him and the force from the shot pushed him to the ground. His gun fell out of his hand and slid across the floor. He clutched his chest and moaned in pain while feeling for his weapon with his free hand. He looked up and suddenly there were red dots all around him. Chance rolled over several times until he crashed into a stack of wooden pallets sitting on the floor. He took cover behind them and tried to radio dispatch again. One of the bullets missed his head by a centimeter and hit his radio, shattering it into pieces.

"Shit!" he yelled and pressed his face to the floor and wrapped his arms around the back of his head.

The shooting stopped and he glanced up. Several red dots were moving closer to him. He could hear the men with the guns whispering to one another. One said that he thought he had shot him. The other wanted to make sure. The dots bounced around coming closer and closer. Chance looked around for an escape route, but didn't want to give his position away.

He squeezed his eyes shut and prayed silently. *Please, God! Don't let me die like this! Forgive me for everything I've done!* He was trying to keep it together, but a tear escaped and dripped onto the cold, hard floor. He thought about April and wished he hadn't been away from her recently. He wondered how she would react to the news of his death. He could hear the mens' feet shuffling right in front of him. This was it.

Without warning several men burst through the open front door and began firing. The men that had tried to kill Chance fired back, but were outnumbered. They started backing out the rear of the building as the new arrivals came forward. Once all of them were inside, they pressed harder until the original aggressors fled out the back door. Chance was shaking. The new arrivals had flipped on flashlights and he could see that they were all dressed in all black tactical gear. He wished he would have ran the other way while they were occupied. The sound of one of the men walking toward him echoed through the empty building. Chance closed his eyes and prepared for impact.

"Get up. Let's get out of here." He recognized the voice of the man standing over him with his hand outstretched.

"Tariq? What are you doing here?" He slowly rose to his feet, confused as to what was happening.

"He's here to make sure you stay alive."

Chance looked at the man who had spoken up. "Rahim? What the hell is going on?"

"Tariq knew something was about to go down when they put you on nights. It looks like your partners in blue don't think you're a valuable member of the team."

Chance's eyes bulged and he blinked over and over. It was hard to digest that the people he had been working with for years had tried to kill him. He shook his head back and forth.

Tariq stepped forward and placed a hand on his shoulder. "I know it's a lot to take in, bro. No time to do that here. Let's get out of here before they come back and succeed.

They all exited the building cautiously. Chance absentmindedly rubbed his chest.

"Did they hit you?" Tariq asked.

"Yeah, but I had my vest on."

They each let out a grateful sigh before embracing and heading in separate directions.

As Chance fled the scene, he dialed his father. He needed some solid advice right now.

Mr. Carrington picked up seemingly wide awake.

"Dad! I'm in trouble. I need your help!"

"I've spoken with Grayson and he told me what's going on with you, Chance. You let me down. You and I have nothing to say to one another."

He hung up.

The news alert woke both April and Charlotte up. It was part of their jobs to always be aware of what was going on in the city, so they looked over at each other and chuckled when both of the phones rang out simultaneously.

April stared at the phone as the word scrolled across her screen. *Officer missing and feared dead.* She didn't need to read the rest of the story to know it was Chance. She clicked on the video and Rocky was on the scene speaking with reporters. He said that the police car had been found a couple of miles away, but there was no sign of Chance. He sniffled and covered his eyes, seemingly devastated by the disappearance of his former partner.

"Not a damn tear in sight," April fumed.

Both she and Charlotte threw back the comforter and leapt to their feet. All the movement roused Janice, who had stretched out across the foot of the bed.

"What going on?" she asked groggily.

"Something has happened to Chance. I'm going to go find out what." April answered as she slipped into her jeans and t-shirt and put on her running shoes.

"You're not going anywhere by yourself. I'm coming with you!" Janice offered. She didn't bother changing out of her long john pajamas. She put on her slippers and a light jacket and was ready to go.

"I'm coming, too," Charlotte added, pulling a sweater over her head.

The ladies rushed out of the bedroom and down the hallway toward the underground parking garage. April had taken notice of the wall of keys to all of the cars in the lot. There would definitely have a ride out of here. They stepped into the elevator and descended to the garage. As the doors opened, Tariq, Rahim and the security team appeared.

"What's going on? Where are y'all going?" Rahim demanded.

April got in his face. "You tell me, what's going on. Chance is missing and you all are walking in here dressed like... this." She looked the men up and down. They looked as if they had just come off an undercover mission. All of them had assault rifles strapped to their backs and handguns holstered at their waists. She pulled out a knife, prepared to gut Rahim if she had to.

Tariq stepped in between them. "April, stop. It's not what you think."

Still holding her knife up, she turned to him. "Oh, yeah? Then what is it, Riq?

"After running into Chance at the police station, Rahim and I figured there was some funny shit going down. We decided to keep an eye out for him. He got a bogus call to an abandoned building where Rocky and his boys tried to kill him. We came in, got them up off him and made sure he got out of there alive."

Her eyes were glossy. "Did you? Did you get him out… alive?"

"We did. He took a shot to the chest, but had on his vest. He's good."

She let out the breath she was holding. Charlotte and Janice both grabbed their chests, relieved at the news.

"Where is he? Is he with you?" She looked around the men into the garage.

"Nah. He went his way and we went ours."

With that April brushed past them, grabbed a set of keys and motioned for Charlotte and Janice to get into the SUV with her.

"Wait. You can't go out. If they tried to take out one of their own, what you think they'll do to you?" Rahim grabbed April by the arm to stop her.

She looked down at his hand on her arm then gave him a dirty look. He instinctively let go and the ladies loaded into the car, drove up the ramp toward the exit and out of the garage.

Once they were out of sight, Tariq turned to Rahim, who made eye contact with his head of security. He barked some orders to his crew and the entire team got into vehicles and sped out of the garage. Rahim and Tariq headed into the building.

"How are you going to find him?" Charlotte wrinkled her forehead, concern written all over her face.

"I know exactly where he is." April admitted as she sped up and down back streets.

Janice perked up and squinted her eyes at her sister. "Wait. What you mean you know exactly where he is?"

April huffed. She wasn't in the mood to explain, but knew Jan would not quit asking until she knew. "Awhile back, Rocky messed over the wrong dude. Chance happened to be with him, so the guy supposedly put a hit out on both of them." Janice and Charlotte gasped. April rolled her eyes, regretting that she had shared, but continued. "Chance was worried that they may somehow find out where we lived, so, we bought a second property that no one knew about to be used in case of emergency."

Janice's mouth hung open. She and her sister didn't keep secrets. She wondered how April could have kept this from her. Charlotte broke her bitter trance by speaking up.

"So the bad guys don't know about this spot... but what about Rocky? I'm sure he knows where to find Chance."

April shook her head back and forth as she bent a corner on two wheels. "No. He was always a risk. We figured if he got caught up, he may give Chance's location away in a minute to save his own ass." She could feel both women's piercing eyes locked on her but neither said a word.

Finally, they pulled up to a gated community and April rolled her window down and punched in a code. The gates swung open long enough for them to speed through before closing behind them. Once inside, the vehicle crept along slowly, April surveying the neighborhood to make sure nothing was amiss. Satisfied that the community was still sleeping, she pulled to the curb and parked the SUV. All of them emerged and closed the doors quietly. She motioned for them to follow her and they all tiptoed to the next block. They stopped in front of a small rambler. April stopped to look at the two cars in the driveway. One was Chance's but the other, she had never seen. The hairs immediately stood up on the back of her neck and she slinked toward the front porch with her sister and friend on her heels. They could see the dim living room lamp shining through the sheer curtain on the front window. They stepped onto the creaky porch and April walked over and peered in. At first what she saw didn't register, then she gasped and stumbled. Frightened by her reaction, Charlotte stepped back off of the porch but Janice rushed to April's side to look for herself. Chance was sitting on a stool with his shirt off and a woman stood in front of him with a hand on his chest, rubbing gently.

"Son of a bitch!" Janice growled through gritted teeth. She turned to walk off and tripped over a flower pot sending it across the porch.

Chance and the woman both turned toward the window. Within a second, he had his handgun out and aimed directly at them. April grabbed her sister by the arm and ducked out of range. They ran off the porch and dashed down the sidewalk. Chance burst out the door and gave chase.

"Stop or I'll shoot!"

Charlotte and Janice froze, leaving April no choice but to face him.

He walked up and they turned to greet him. Shock washed over his face. "April! What are you doing here? I wasn't expecting you."

"Obviously," she mumbled, nodding at the woman who had followed Chance outside and stood behind him.

He followed her eyes to the woman and spun back to face her. "Wait. What? It's not what you think, April."

She folded her arms across her chest. Janice could no longer contain herself. "We can see exactly what's going on. Don't lie to my sister!"

Chance ignored her. "April, you know me--"

"She doesn't know a damn thing! Who the hell is this?" Janice demanded, getting into his face.

"Shut up, Jan!" he yelled.

She became incensed and drew back to slap him. April grabbed her hand and stopped her. "Jan, don't. He's not even worth it."

Janice reluctantly relaxed her arm. April grabbed her and Charlotte by the hands and led them back to the car.

"April. Can I talk to you for a minute? Please?"

"About what, Chance? Clearly, there's nothing you need from me." She slid into the driver's seat and slammed the door.

He walked up and knocked on the window. She sped off leaving him and the woman staring after her.

She wiped away the tears blurring her vision as she sped back toward safety.

"Who was she?" Janice asked.

"That was Candice Reynolds." April laughed.

Charlotte eyes rounded. "Candice Reynolds? The Chief of Police?"

"The one and only." April confirmed.

Janice and Charlotte both went limp relaxing into the leather seats. April rolled down the windows and let the dawn air blow in her face all the way back to Rahim's place.

WANTED

None of them could believe this was happening. April watched as her face popped up on the television screen. "Could they have used a worst picture?" she fumed.

Janice pounded the table. Her sister had always been the good girl that followed the rules. If anybody should be under suspicion for anything it should be her.

"These snakes! I can't believe they are doing this to you! How can we fight back?"

Rahim walked in and interjected. "We fight back by gathering our own evidence and going to the news with it. We also need to get the attention of the Feds. The whole department is corrupt and needs to be taken down."

Everyone nodded in agreement. They had all been working for days to build a case against the police. After being chased down and almost arrested, April knew things were coming to a head. She'd had the foresight to move all of her firm's records to a secure facility off-site. When the firm burst in and rummaged through her files, all they took away was blank pages and unrelated documents she had collected from the recycling center. She knew they would be even more upset that she had fooled them and would be out to get her by any means. But to insinuate that she was a person of interest in an embezzlement scheme was lower than she'd ever expected them to go.

Her phone vibrated and she glanced at it. Tariq had given her a new phone at the hospital and she regretted giving Chance the number. Ever since she had caught him at their hideaway with Candice Reynolds, he'd rang her relentlessly. When she didn't answer, he sent text messages. He tried unsuccessfully to convince April not to believe her own eyes. He claimed that the Chief of Police was there on work-related matters and that she was looking at his chest to make sure the bullet had not gone through the vest, which made him even more unbelievable. How could he show her where their secret spot was? She was at the top of the organization that had just tried to execute him. *He must really be feeling her,* April thought.

Today was the start of Rocky's trial for planting evidence on Tariq. April knew the department had tried their best to ensure that this day would never come. They'd had too many scandals to count over the years and one more would certainly result in federal oversight and an overhaul of the whole department. They were willing to do whatever it took to stop her.

She stood in the living room in her best kick-ass prosecuting attire; a mid-length black pencil skirt and a sheer black button-up blouse, paid with five-inch black leather heels.

"You look like you're on the way to a funeral," Janice joked.

"I am. I'm about to bury Rocky Moretti," she replied with a straight face.

She looked at her watch. "Where is Riq? He's supposed to be here."

Right on cue, Tariq walked in. He too was dressed in all black and looked as if he was ready for war. "You rang, sis?"

"Yes. Where've you been? Is everything okay?"

He smiled. "Everything is better than okay. I was laying some groundwork. I want to be ready for whatever happens today." He walked up and took both of her hands into his, staring into her eyes. "You know they're going to be all over you as soon as you walk in. Are you ready?"

She nodded and swallowed the lump of fear that was trapped in her throat. They all piled into the waiting vehicles and headed toward the courthouse.

The courthouse was jam-packed. April approached the entrance and felt like everyone was staring at them. Three of Rahim's security detail led the way. Charlotte and Janice walked right next to her in lock step. Rahim, Tariq and three more security guards followed closely behind. She should have felt well protected, but April knew that the only people that could take weapons through the metal detectors would be the police. Inside, she would be dependent on pure physicality to keep her from harm.

They all made their way through the courthouse security and April finally set up at the prosecution table. Charlotte sat next to her and everyone else accompanying them sat on the bench immediately behind them. She looked over at the defense table and immediately recognized Rocky's would-be attorney. She had been on the opposite side of the courtroom from him on numerous occasions. She seemed to be the police department's go-to gal when one their officers was accused of wrongdoing.

She pulled files out of her briefcase and noticed that her hands were shaking. In all the cases that April had tried, she exuded confidence and preparedness. Today was different. There was more on the line than her reputation and she had to admit to herself that for once, she was scared. She looked back at the gallery and made eye contact with Janice and Tariq. They both smiled reassuringly. She forced a smile back.

The courtroom quickly filled up. As expected, a ton of spectators and supporters of Rocky filled the benches on the other side. She noted that a number of people she'd represented in police brutality cases and their families sat directly behind her, all wanting to see Rocky finally punished for his corruption. A few news organizations lined the section that had been designated for the press. They whispered amongst themselves about the upcoming proceedings. Notably missing was any sign of Rocky or his cohorts. Typically, in these cases, the accused officers and his co-workers were early, entering with bells and whistles. It was more of an intimidation tactic than anything. The fact that they had not shown up yet made April unsettled. She could feel that something wasn't right. She checked her watch and it was 8:30 on the dot.

The judge entered the courtroom clearly agitated with all of the fanfare and the incessant chattering from the crowd. "Order in the courtroom!" he ordered, banging his gavel loudly on the bench.

The room fell silent. April barely listened as he went through his preliminary instructions and questioned the defense as to the whereabouts of their client. They asked for a few more minutes to allow Rocky to arrive and the judge granted the request before returning to his chambers.

April flipped through the pages in her file once more. It was all there; witness statements, pictures from private investigators, even the recording of Rocky confessing during the traffic stop. It would be an open and shut case. She glanced at the time again; 8:40. *This is unbelievable! I could never be late like this and get away with it.* She thought.

"You good, April?" Charlotte placed a hand on hers.

"Oh. Yeah. I'm good, just going over everything again."

Tariq and Janice walked over and began chatting. April was glad they did because every second that ticked by made her more and more anxious.

All of a sudden, both doors to the courtroom swung open. Everyone in attendance turned to see who had entered. Several officers swarmed in and headed in April's direction. Her heart raced and her head was spinning. Tariq stood in front of her while Charlotte and Janice moved to her sides quickly. Rahim and his team all stood and cut off the path to the prosecution table.

"Step aside," Lt. Grayson barked.

Rahim showed no signs of being intimidated. "I will not step aside. What do you want?"

Lt. Grayson turned his nose up and balled his fist. "Not that it's any of your business, Mr. Salek. We're here to take Ms. Story in for questioning surrounding her firm."

Rahim laughed. "You and I know that's absolute bullshit. You're here to stop Ms. Story from exposing your department. We won't allow it."

Lt. Grayson's nostrils flared. He narrowed his eyes and stepped forward. "Step aside, or we will put you aside, Mr. Salek," he spat.

The gallery gasped and the flash of cameras popped all around them.

"Well, that's exactly what you're going to have to do, then," Rahim shot back as he stepped closer to the lieutenant.

April lunged forward. There was no way she was going to let Rahim and his men end up hurt or worse on her behalf.

"It's okay, Rahim. I'll go with them."

Tariq yanked her back toward him. "You will not go with them. They already tried to get rid of you, April. What you think they're gonna do when you ride off with them alone? They ain't taking you nowhere."

The lieutenant turned to his men. "Take her and anyone who gets in the way into custody!"

The officers all converged on them. Rahim's men started tussling with them to hold them at bay. Rocky stepped from the back. He pulled his gun and aimed it directly at Rahim. Everyone in the crowd took cover.

"No!" April jumped in front of him.

Rocky bit his bottom lip hard. His finger hovered over the trigger. April could see his disdain from her in every fiber of his being. He looked around and the cameras trained on him and opted not to shoot her in public, but kept his gun pointed, waiting on a reason.

Now the crowd had gotten involved. Both sides were hurling insults at one another and some had begun to push and shove. She looked around the courtroom, unable to believe things had gotten to this place.

Without warning, the doors burst open again. This time, a flood of federal agents spilled into the courtroom. Everyone stopped in their tracks and looked around, confused. The men walked over and began taking the police officers into custody. Rocky protested as one of them took his firearm and placed his hands behind his back. After all his men had been cuffed, the lieutenant fumed.

"Who is in charge here?" He demanded.

An agent stepped forward. "I am."

"What is going on? Let my men go!"

"Afraid I can't do that, sir," he replied. He nodded to one of his agents who came over and forced the lieutenant's hands behind his back.

"You... and your men are under arrest for conspiracy to commit murder."

The officers were speechless as the agents led them out of the courtroom. Chance walked in with one of the agents while Rocky was being taken away. As they crossed paths, Rocky struggled to get to him.

"You're a fucking traitor!" he snarled.

Chance stared him down unflinching. "You try to kill me, but I'm the traitor, Roc?" he laughed.

The agent forced Rocky out of the courtroom. April stood stunned. She couldn't find any words to say in the moment. Chance approached and Tariq stepped up. The men embraced and thanked each other. April looked at Tariq for answers, but he just smiled.

"I told you I would lookout, sis."

Chance walked over and stood in front of April, extending his open arms. She was still angry and wanted him to know it. She thought about leaving him standing there. Instead she collapsed into his arms and began to sob. He held her for a long time, murmuring words of comfort to her. When she finally pulled herself together, she stepped away.

"So what's up, Chance? Is my sister still a wanted woman?" Janice asked, her arms folded across her chest and her stance defiant.

He chuckled. Right now he could really appreciate her overprotective nature. "No, Jan. Everything is good. Those guys will never bother any of us again."

Rahim walked over and shook Chance's hand, thanking him for everything he had done. Everyone said their goodbyes and left the courthouse with cameras flashing and reporters with microphones clamoring for a statement.

Before getting into his car, Chance turned toward April. "Hey!" he yelled.

"Yeah," she answered putting a hand above her eyes to shield them from the shining sun.

"Can I call you tonight?"

She thought about it for a moment. "You can try." She slid into the backseat of the SUV with Charlotte and Janice.

"That's cold, April," Charlotte said.

The car sped back toward Rahim's building.

"I know you miss him. Just call him," Janice groaned when she tired of watching April flip through the channels.

They were spending Friday evening with their parents who had just returned from their extended vacation. Three months had passed since Rocky had been taken off the streets and life had returned to normal.

Right after the arrests, Chance had tried over and over to meet up. He said he missed April and wanted to explain the circumstances of his involvement with the Chief of Police. In April's opinion, there was nothing he could say to her that would make sense, so she ignored him. With him still working under the woman he had an affair with, there would never be any hope for their relationship.

"I do miss him. Not enough to let him sell me a bag of lies."

Janice stood up. "But how do you know he is going to lie to you? The man saved your life. Don't you think you should hear him out?"

April looked at her with skepticism. "Gee, I don't know, Jan. Would you hear your man out after you saw a woman rubbing on his shirtless chest?"

"Hell no!" Both women busted out laughing.

"And since when did you become such a big fan of Chance's?"

"I didn't say all that now. I do respect the man, though. It took a lot of courage to do what he did. After all, he is the reason my sister is right here with me. How can I not like him?"

"Hmmm." April stood to leave. "I need to go find a dress for tomorrow's ceremony."

"Alright. Have fun." Janice waved.

"Are we gonna see you there?" Tariq asked.

April sighed. "Yes, Riq. I'll be there."

Tonight was a special black tie event the city had decided to put on to raise money for new programs. With the arrest of half of the police department and the FBI combing through the city's criminal justice practices with a fine-toothed comb, the Chief of Police had done a complete overhaul. Officers had been required to complete additional de-escalation and diversity training. New officers had been hired to police the communities they actually lived in. The initiative for fining officers who purposely turned off their body cam had been introduced and passed. An outreach project that would connect the officers with the taxpayers they worked for was underway. Rahim had been called in to help spearhead the process and he had hired Tariq as his right-hand man. Now, instead of Our Lives Matter being a perceived thorn in the side of law enforcement, they worked hand-in-glove to prevent some of the issues they had previously protested. April smiled when she thought about how far they had come.

At the fundraising dinner, the Mayor would finally let the public in on what they were working on behind the scenes. Now that the police force had hired enough employees, they would announce who would be occupying the most prominent positions. Although former Lieutenant Grayson had shot down Chance's opportunity to be Assistant Chief of Police, April was certain that after all he had done, he would be at least promoted to lieutenant.

She looked at herself in the mirror, satisfied with her choice of outfit. The little black dress was short and flirty, but still classy. Her high heels added a sexy touch and her sleek updo finished the look. A horn honked outside. She looked out and saw Charlotte waiting. Grabbing her clutch, she ran out the door.

There was no shortage of wealthy socialites on hand.

"They're going to raise a lot of money tonight," Charlotte mused when they entered the foyer and looked out over the dining room.

They walked toward the spiral staircase heading down to take their seats. April was so busy trying to keep from toppling down the stairs in her stilettos, she didn't see Chance walking up.

"Can I help you down the stairs?" he asked, holding out his elbow.

"Sure, I guess." She hooked her arm through his and let him lead her down the long stairs. Charlotte smiled giddily.

Chance was dressed in an all-black tailored Christian Dior suit, paired with an all-white button up shirt and a black tie with thin silver stripes. April hadn't laid eyes on him in months and had forgotten how good he looked. His light Burberry cologne awakened her senses and his freshly tapered fade made her imagine running her fingers over his waves. He glanced back at her and caught her staring. She wanted to kick herself when he smiled to himself.

"You look beautiful, April."

"Thank you. You look nice as well."

When they got to the dining area, he asked her where she was sitting and she pointed to her assigned seat.

"Wow. I'm at the table next to yours," he sang.

They continued to her table, where he pulled out her chair. Before walking off, he kissed her hand, leaving her body tingling from the warm touch of his lips. She couldn't take her eyes off of him as he walked the short distance to his own table and sat down. Something was different about him; his stride was confident and aside from his apparent desire for her, this was the first time April had really seen him look genuinely happy.

Her eyes widened when she realized that Tariq, Rahim and their ladies had been seated at the table with Chance. They were all watching her watch him with delighted faces. She quickly flipped them all the middle finger and turned away, tuning out their laughter.

"Chance is looking fine as hell," Janice said, slipping into her chair.

"We know. April couldn't take her eyes off of him," Charlotte joked.

April punched her in the arm playfully. "Oh, please. I was not sweating him."

"Umhmmm," both ladies said in unison.

"Well, he sure is sweating you," Janice nodded in his direction.

Chance had turned his chair slightly and was watching April. She looked behind her to see if he was looking at something else. *Nope. Staring right at me,* she thought. She tried to look back at him just as long and hard to make him uncomfortable, but he kept looking. She squirmed under his gaze and was relieved when the waiter arrived with dinner. After they started eating she glanced over at him and was elated, but bewildered to see him engaged in a lighthearted conversation with Rahim and Tariq. The way they were interacting, if she didn't know any better, she'd believe they all were the best of friends.

The waiters picked up the dishes after everyone had finished and the jazz music playing in the background stopped. The host took the stage to greet and thank everyone for being here. After he said a few words he introduced the Mayor who went over new projects and initiatives. April was anxious to hear his announcements about who would be doing what in the police department.

"I know you all expected me to talk about the law enforcement staffing, but I thought it would be best coming from our new Chief of Police. Welcome Candice Reynolds to the stage!"

The audience clapped and cheered. April felt a lump in her throat. Her hand felt sweaty wrapped around her glass of wine. As the woman walked across the stage, April gulped down the remaining wine in the glass. *Get a hold of yourself, April. Of course she would be here. She's the Chief of Police.* Her self-talk wasn't working. Even months later, the thought of being in the same room with the woman Chance had been involved with knocked her off kilter. As the woman reached the podium and smiled, April imagined punching her right in the face. She looked over at Chance who was smiling and clapping and couldn't help but feel jealous.

"Thank you, Mayor. As you all know, I am Candice Reynolds, your new Chief of Police..." She went into her bio and April looked on wondering what Chance could have seen in the woman. She was pretty enough, but seemed uncomfortable in the evening gown she wore. When she had walked across the stage it seemed as if wearing heels were foreign to her.

"Taking this position was a big move and sacrifice for my family..." April frowned, wondering why this woman who had a family had chosen to have an affair with a subordinate. "I own all of my success to my wife. Gina, stand up." Her wife rose and the crowd clapped and cheered. April wanted to sink into the floor. Janice lightly kicked her leg over and over, making sure she had heard the revelation.

After the noise subsided, she continued on. "It's not often that you find good people, willing to do the right thing, even at their own risk. My new Assistant Chief of Police is one of a rare breed. He risked his life, his career and his reputation to do what was right. When he came to me and told me what was going on in the department, I found it hard to believe. It couldn't have been easy to stand up against the wrong he'd witnessed, but he trusted me and with his leadership we have ridded our police department of the corrupt officers that were polluting our community and our justice system. Ladies and gentlemen, it's my pleasure to introduce my new Assistant Chief of police, Chance Carrington!"

The entire room rose to their feet cheering and clapping as Chance approached the stage. April was awestruck. Everything was moving in slow motion. He climbed the stairs and made his way to the podium, shaking the Chief's hand as she exited.

Chance stood there looking out over the crowd. His eyes welled with tears of joy. Seeing him up there, April couldn't hold back her tears either. She grabbed a napkin of the table and dabbed the corners of her eyes.

He cleared his throat. "All my life I've wanted this. I wanted this for the notoriety. I wanted this to please my father. I wanted this to prove that I was worthy." The audience sat silent. "Those were the wrong reasons for wanting this. A little over four years ago, I met someone... someone who would change my life forever. This person was passionate about doing the right thing and standing up for what you believe in. She taught me that money, popularity and a title mean nothing if you are not doing the right thing. She taught me that you have to be strong in your beliefs and stand by them, even if it means losing something important to you. By not bowing down to my demands that she be more like me, she changed me into a person like her. I stand here today, happy to accept this position as Assistant Chief of Police, ecstatic for the opportunity to stand up for what I believe in and to do what is right for all of us. I owe my success to one woman. April Story. April, can you please come up here?"

She cupped her hands over her mouth and her feet felt like lead. Tariq and Rahim yelled out for her to go up there and Janice pushed her forward.

"Girl, if you don't go get your man..." she prodded.

April walked up to the stage, trembling. When she reached Chance he embraced her and kissed her as if no one else were in the room. She wrapped her arms around his neck and kissed him back. The crowded erupted. Chance released her and asked for quiet.

"Chance, I'm so sorry. I should have heard you out. I--"

"Shhh." He placed a finger over her mouth. "None of that matters, baby. We are here now. That's all that counts."

"I want the world to know how much you mean to me and how much I love you." He knelt down on one knee. "April Story, will you marry me?" He pulled a small felt jewelry box out of his inside pocket and flashed a gleaming diamond ring. She was speechless.

"Say, yes!" Charlotte yelled out.

Everyone in the building laughed.

"Yes, Chance. Yes, I'll marry you," April answered through tears. He put the ring on her finger and stood up to kiss her again.

The whole room hooted and hollered. He took her by the hand and led her off the stage. When they walked past all of the dining tables and up the stairs toward the exit, April frowned as she looked at him. She dug her heels into the step.

"Wait, Chance! Where are we going?"

He turned to face her. "First, I'm about to take you home, rip this dress off of you and make love to you. Then me and my little superwoman are going to clean up this entire city and take over the world." His eyes gleamed.

April smiled to herself and followed his lead.

THE END

Have you read my other books?

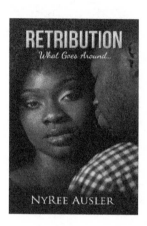

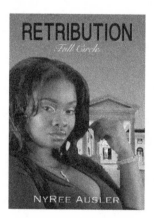

Available on Amazon!

9 781791 631390